George Francis Savage-Armstrong

Poems

Lyrical and Dramatic

George Francis Savage-Armstrong

Poems
Lyrical and Dramatic

ISBN/EAN: 9783744793612

Printed in Europe, USA, Canada, Australia, Japan

Cover: Foto ©Andreas Hilbeck / pixelio.de

More available books at **www.hansebooks.com**

P O E M S :

LYRICAL AND DRAMATIC.

BY

GEORGE FRANCIS ARMSTRONG, M.A.,

PROFESSOR OF HISTORY AND ENGLISH LITERATURE

IN THE QUEEN'S COLLEGE, CORK.

A NEW EDITION.

LONDON:

LONGMANS, GREEN, READER, AND DYER.

1873.

CONTENTS.

SLAIN IN THE FOREFRONT.

H E is down in the battle,
     The foremost to fall,
The loved of our host,
     Whom *I* loved more than all.
The golden-brown hair
     In the battle-dust lies ;
The black silken lashes
     Droop o'er the great eyes ;
To the full, fringèd lips
     Clings a smile ; like a streak
Of a sunset the life-tint
     Still rests on his cheek.

' His life is not wasted,'
     God calleth to me :
' The battle rolls onward :
     His spirit is free.
For the freer life fought he,
     Fought well, and has won

What the battle-host strove for
  That still shall strive on.
Come *thou* from the rearward,
  Step forth to his place,
Lift off the stout armour,
  The helmet unlace,
Make fast the stained corslet
  Around thine own breast,
About thine own temples
  Bind morion and crest,
Upraise the fallen buckler,
  Take thou the red sword—
The dead hand that grasps it
  Will yield at *thy* word ;
And sigh not, and grieve not,
  Nor turn left or right,
But, strong and undaunted,
  Move on to the fight.'

I've ta'en helm and buckler
  Of him my soul loved,
Put on the whole armour
  The brave one has proved,
Stept out to the forefront,
  And stand as he stood,
When arrayed for the onset
  He spilt his warm blood.

And his soul with my soul
  In the long eager strife
Shall nerve arm and hand
  With a life more than life ;
With a force not mine only,
  As blow follows blow,
Every stroke of his good sword
  Shall sweep on the foe ;
And the might of his great heart
  With mine shall be blent,
Till the last power is ebbed,
  And all energy spent,
And I drift through the gloom
  Firm of hope, high of cheer,
To the land where he roameth,
  My soul's pioneer.

SUNDERED FRIENDSHIP.

MUST we part thus, with even so light a touch
  Of hands, and so cold murmuring of lips,
    Nor dare lift up our faces, lest our eyes
  Meet once, and as a stream of moonlight slips
    Drenching the broken cloud and muffled skies
Storm-blown, the soul through yearning overmuch

B 2

Outshed itself? nor tell to one another
How dear the life was that hath end to-night,
  Nor drink one pure sad kiss, as child or mother,
We who have loved as child or mother might?

What had they whispered had I laid mine arm
  Under the streaming darkness of thy hair,
    Drawn thee beside my bosom tenderly,
  With tears of sorrow and words of weak despair
    Blest thee and taken sad farewell of thee,
Leaning my lips a moment on the warm
  Flushed cheek uplifted ; rather than repressing
My spirit's gentle love of thee, I stilled
  Mine agony, and without word of blessing,
Or tear, or sigh, passed from thee mute and chilled?

I sought thee not for touch of toying hand,
  Or pressure of lip, whose lips were fair to kiss,
    Whose hands were clear as carven lily-flowers;
  I sought thee not for any spousal-bliss :
    Ah, if amid thy laughter in light hours
When thy mouth smiled and all thy face was bland,
  I had seized thee in the storm of thy pure glad-
      ness,
For kisses and soft words, as lovers may,
  I wis I should have held thee half in sadness,
Even as one pitying clasps a child at play.

I loved thee for that dear deep lovingness
  Resting within thy tender-brooding eyes ;
    I loved thee for thy wealth of womanhood ;
    Thy quiet questionings, thy sweet replies ;
    Thy patient brows that knew no bitter mood ;
Thy mouth's compression, telling of distress
  Held by the throat in strength of self-devotion,
Hard duties borne and love unconquered ;
  Not for thy footstep's gentle stately motion,
Nor the proud pose of thine imperial head.

Ah, sitting at thy side, I felt that God
  Slept not nor had forgot us in disdain ;
    Ah, sitting in the hearing of thy breath,
    I gave God thanks for life and sorrow and pain,
    And smiled upon the livid frown of death,
And dreaded not the foldings of the sod,
  Nor the far shadow of the dim hereafter,
Nor any clouds that darken or efface—
  Sitting within the hearing of thy laughter,
And gazing at God's light upon thy face.

Ah, when the little children round thee prest,
  Caught at thy skirts and beat thee on the cheek,
    And called thee tender little baby-names,
    Thou smiling down upon them mild and meek,
    My heart forgot its narrow earthly aims,

I felt the great sobs rising in my breast,
  I could have bowed before thy knees in sorrow,
And wept till every pang had passed and died:
  From thy great heart my poorer heart would
    borrow
New strength of love to cheer me and to guide.

We shall not ever wander in the woods
  Once more, or laugh together, or clasp hands
    Going and coming; nay, the merry jest
  Shall be a thing unspoken, like hid lands
    That blossom for no eyes, lying at rest,
Or sparkle and glimmer of unholden goods
  Where no hand lives to clutch them; we shall
    listen
Never again together to low sighs
  Æolian when winds breathe and soft stars glisten,
Nor watch again the sunset-stained skies.

All is gone over, and thy life will run
  Even as ere my coming; thou wilt clasp
    A hundred hands, and feel mine nevermore
  Woven in thine with loyal reverent grasp;
    Treading of many a foot about thy door
Will thrill thee, never of that familiar one
  Dead summers had made dearest; friend and
    lover

Will look into thy face, but among men,
   That one man's eyes wherein thou couldst
      discover
Thy soul's own soul, shall reach thee not again.

Awhile thou wilt come back to me with drift
   Of the sea's breath; ay, with the cuckoo's plaint;
      With snatches of sad music or of sweet;
      With gleams of sun on mountain heights; and
       quaint
      Odour of warm rare blooms; and rhythmic beat
Of happy dances: suddenly as shift
   Clouds from autumnal stars, or in the branches
Leap with light feet the winds amid the leaves,
   Thou wilt come back to me, as the moon quenches
Her glory, or at sad dawns, or silent eves.

And all my heart will yearn and give God praise,
   Seeing thee nigh, and tears of dear delight
      Will rise and choke the full soul's utterance,
   And swift as the cloud blots the stars of night,
      Or the wind lulls amid the leaves, the trance
That bore thee back will fade, and the old days
   With love and rest will be a hueless vision,
And the bleak mist will fold me like a spell,
   Dead mouths leer round about me in derision,
Dead faces flash against me out of hell.

Awhile thou wilt weep gentle tears in vain,
  Remembering happy laughter in the leas;
    The shadow crossing o'er the gravel walk
  Will draw thee to thy window; cadences
    Of manly voices heard in blended talk
Will startle thee and wring thy heart with pain;
  At turnings of the street thine eyes will wander,
Seeking for one who comes not in the throngs;
  Over thy hand's work thou wilt droop to ponder,
And pause to sigh amid thy merriest songs.

Thy dresses will hold memories of me;
  Thou wilt lay by a ribbon or a flower
    To bring back thoughts of me—'for this he
      chanced
  To give me, drenched with April's dewy dower;
    And this I wore one happy time we danced
Together on a night of jubilee.'
  Thou wilt not wear thy hair flung back un-
      braided,
Adown thy neck, lest even so slight a thing
  Looked at should hurt thee with a pleasure
      faded:
Thou wilt not gladden with the dawn of spring.

Awhile, and all will sicken like a dream—
  Ay, Time will draw thee from me, as the sea

Draws weed or shell flung up from glutted
   graves
To the starved sand, and runs in mockery
   Back, laughing in the hollows of his waves ;
Awhile, and all will sicken like a dream,
   And though I stretch wild arms, and follow crying
Down the steep shores, and calling on thy name,
   There will come nought but noise, and the wind
      flying,
And buffetings to bruise me and to maim.

Out of the gulfs Time rendereth not his prey.
   I will go wandering up and down till all
      Anger and bitterness be spent, and strength
   Fail utterly, and sorrow's sweetness pall—
      Yea, till the joy of sorrow faint at length,
   And all pain's pleasantness be drained away,
      And it seem better and wiser to forget thee
Than nurse a life with withered sorrow fraught,
      To weed thee out of memory, and set thee
A dream among dead dreams that trouble us not.

We shall forget, and deem it happiest
   To have forgotten, finding other loves,
      Finding and losing all our whole lives through :
   For we shall grow too wise, as our sun moves
      Seaward and deathward, even to renew

Old pains of youth to vex a hard-won rest . .
 ' Let youth drift by with all its weary passion : '
Then the hard lips will smile, and all the soul
 Laugh quietly and in a lordly fashion,
Having outlived its hour of heaviest dole.

Forget, forget—ah God, is this life's end,
 To love, and lose, and weep, and laugh at tears?
 Is there too much of love in the world, that men
 Must curse it so, and let the hurrying years
 Sweep over it in ruin ? Is there, then,
No lack of love to succour and befriend,
 Or need of it to lighten and to leaven
Life and the spites and griefs and hates therein,
 But earth must crush the purest flower of heaven,
Branding it, as God brands the flower of sin ?

It would not understand, it would not wait;
 The world must sin or slay—and so hath slain,
 And sinned in slaying, that high love of ours ;
 It could not watch us loving and not stain
 Its hands with hues of bruisèd poison-flowers
Polluted, being skilled to imitate
 Foul ways, and with a heart athirst to cherish
Foul dreams of sin where sin is none to find ;
 So, for the great world's good we bleed and perish,
Maiden, because the world is foul and blind.

O come to me, come back across the night,
Dear human soul that smiled but yester-morn
Through soft sad eyes upon me, loving me ;
Dear human hands which God hath framed to
adorn
Earth with their beauty, touch me trustfully,
Stretching mine own out desolate ! . . What blight
Hath God thrown down on our abiding-places,
Or what fell sin hath man found power to do,
That we must shun the light of dearest faces
Lest new sin thrive of loving leal and true ? . .

'Tis well, dear heart—'tis best—we know not all :
Let them go by, the world and sin and love.
I marvel what the Father keeps for us,
Beyond the great wide sea where the winds
rove
Lonely, and never ship hath sailed, who thus
Have seen love fade in us, and droop and fall,
And lost the one best gift of life in living,
And emptied all our heart of it, and passed
Out thus into the tracts of darkness, giving
The world its will. What shall be found at last ?

THE INVISIBLE.

WILT thou give no sign, though I call, though I cry
Through the night, O my God, though I seek in
the waste,
In the seas, and my eyes strain up through Thy
wide
Drear heaven ?
O where, in what deep, dread abyss
Of the infinite skies
Dwellest Thou, that the wild long cry of my lips
Pierces nor reaches Thee ?—so far, far,
So far, far off from the mean weak worm
Thou hast made for Thy sport, and forgotten !
                                        My mouth
Is parched with my crying; the jaw hangs down
Through this yearning, this pain ; and my brows
are claspt
As with steel pressed in and in.   But the hours
Roll by in their black dull foam-strewn tide—
On, on—and Thou the Inexorable
From Thy height movest not, nor by hand, nor by
mouth
Sendest down to the poor, frail, blind one here
One little message of peace ;

Thou, who by breath of the wind in the boughs,
Or sighing of grasses, or lisp and shout
And prattle of billow or ripple, or cry
Of mad wild stream in the clefts of the hills,
Where I climb in the morn to behold the red brow
Of the blood-banded sun uprear through the glooms
Of the cloud-wrapt East,
Couldst speak if Thou wouldst, couldst tell to the
    soul
Pain furrowed, what hope in the midst of Thy
    worlds
Of homeless bitter lands and tracts
Of desolate seas, for such as I,
The sin-stained, yet may live : while thus
I creep to the gate of the field where the dead,
The beloved of my breast, lie cold in the earth,
To stand in the night, my hands close locked
To the clammy rails, with sore sad eyes
Gazing up at the pitiless, grey, hard clouds
And the cold, bleak, silent stars.

IESUS HOMINUM SALVATOR.

A LATTER CRUCIFIXION.

CRUCIFY, crucify, crucify.
Out with him straight from the council-hall ;
We have found him worthy of death ;
Say, by what doom shall he die,
This Christ who would reign over all,
This king, this God, as he saith,
Say by what doom shall he fall ?

Crucify, crucify, crucify.
Hath he not said, ' I am king ? '
Who made thee a king over us, thou Christ,
Who made thee a king ?
Yea, for that word thou diest,
Yea, for that lie.
Crucify, crucify.
To whom shall we bow the knees ?
We worship Reason and Truth,
We have bowed to them from our youth,
We will have no king but these :
Art thou a king, in sooth ?

Saith Pilate, whom will ye that I set free ?
Ye know Barabbas, of sinners chief—
Better Barabbas or he ?
Whom shall it be ?
Barabbas, Barabbas—give us the thief.
Crucify, crucify, crucify.
Bring hither the crown for his head,
Bring hither the robe of purple dye,
To array this Lord of the living and dead,
This God most High !

Simon, Simon, carry the cross . .
Hey ! what is it Pilate saith ?
' I have tried and found in him no fault,
No sin that is worthy of death ' . .
Thy laws are not our laws.
Wouldest thou Cæsar exalt ?
Wouldest thou Truth defend ?
Ha ! if thou lettest him free
Thou art not Cæsar's friend :
Away with him, then, to his end.
Prophesy, prophesy, prophesy,
Who was it spat on thee, Christ, but now ?
Who was it spurned at thee ?
Who in their mockery bow ?
Aha ! we would crave thy grace.
Who is it smote thy face ?

Who is it smote thy cheek?
Why feareth the King to speak?

Strip off the royal array,
And clothe him again in his own attire.
Behold this God is a thing of clay:
Our God is a mist, a fire,
A force, a will, a law,
An essence invisible,
An energy—who can tell?
What need of further delay—
Have we not found a flaw?

Lay him along on the cross.
Have ye driven the nails through palms and feet?
Heave softly, then, as is meet;
Heave bravely, now, with a will;
Here on the brow of the hill,
Betwixt the sinners twain,
Heave him aloft in his pain . .
Nay, not to us is the loss:
Let him hang on his cross!

But write not, 'the King of the Jews,'
But that he *said*, 'I am King.'
There is nought better a man can choose
But only by truth to cling!
Write that he *said*, 'I am king.'

Aha, thou Christ, art thou God indeed ?
Then, save thyself in thy need.
Yea, doth Messias bleed ?
Could blood from the Godhead ooze ?
Lo, ye, the King of the Jews !

Now, if he were the Christ of men,
Surely a sign would come.
Hey ? art thou stricken dumb ?
He will answer us not again.
Might we not, might we not yet believe,
Would he but render a fuller sign ?
We thirst not at all for that blood of thine,
Only to Reason cleave :
Wilt thou not render a sign ?

Doth he call Elias ? well, let be—
Elias will come to his aid !
And what if the proof delayed
Be brought to light at the last !
Elias, Elias—why comes not he,
This bearer of tidings vast ?
But they are deceivers both.
So faith in the dust we cast,
And leave him aloft for the world to see,—
A sight to tickle their sloth.

C

What is this that his servants cry,
The wailing women, the men apart
That beat the breast, and stand
Grief-stricken, with frenzied eye ?
' He hath healed the broken heart;
He hath strengthened the feeble hand ;
He hath given as God can give,—
Bread to the hungry breast,
Light to the darkened land ;
He hath made the dead to live ;
He hath soothed the soul that waits
For dawn in the mist and chill,
Saying to sorrow, Be still,
Quelling the pangs of fear.
Ah, cannot ye understand
That only God can fill
The wants that God creates ?
He hath rent the veil of night ;
He hath given us eye and ear
For pleasure, for new delight,
Letting us feel anear
The breath and glory of God,
Spreading in boundless feasts
Knowledge, and wondrous thought,
From the pleasant gardens brought
By the feet of the angels trod.'

Peace: are not we the Priests?
We hold of knowledge the keys;
We can measure the mind of God;
In our hands is the measuring rod;
We stand and keep the door
Of the mystic sanctuaries
Of wisdom, of hidden lore.
What can *ye* know of these?
We are the Priests, ye wot;
We have measured him, body and soul;
We have found him nought but man,
Who has done as the rest have done
Who have laboured under the sun,
And no more than a strong man can.
The tale of his acts?—'Tis a cheat, a lie,
A rhyme on a poet's scroll.
We have measured him, body and soul;
We have done the thing we sought;
What cause for sorrow or ruth?
We have found him worthy to die . .

(And we are the Priests, ye wot:
We worship Reason and Truth.)

At the Sepulchre.

Ah pale grand face wherein the life-tint rests,
Not wholly gone ! ah lips that smile at peace,
Lit as with dawn-light of a glorious dream
Unuttered ! ah great cold perfect brows
Wherefrom death's hand hath smoothed the
    wrinkles out,
Leaving the strong, thought-moulded marble clear !
Ay me, my Lord, thine eyes of love look up,
Brimmed with heaven's blue like living water-
    wells !
They know not death, those eyes that brood in love
On me, thy servant, who am strong at length
To bear the wagging of their scornful heads
Who shoot their lips out in disdain of thee ;
Or why the patient playful smile that lurks
Under the large and heavy-fringèd lids ?
Yea, wilt thou rise and speak, and heal thine
    hands—
Ah God !—that hold thy blood within their palms,
Staining the fair white skin of them ?   They said
' He raised the dead to life,' and I believed :
And they that slew thee flung the taunt at thee,
That even now the mocking hideous cry,
Mixed with their demon laughter, rings and clings

Within my brain, and will not cease or die,
' Himself he cannot save ! come down, O Christ,
Drop from thy cross, aha, and save thyself! '
I stopt mine ears, and fled far off for pain :
I thought, ' yea, surely at the last my Lord
Will come thence, walking through the midst of
    them,
As through the waves of Galilee he came
That night the fishers tell of up and down ;
Or else his servants will arise and smite,
And make him king indeed, and he will war
And slay and take revenge ; ' and then I stole
Back to the Mount in fear, and heard the last
Wild awful cry of thee, to God, methought,
That ran across the gathering night, and tore
Up through the heavens a path unto his ear
Who sits upon His throne and hears.
                                    And what
Was left for me, but just to take it down—
This body which was thine—and bind thy head
Thus ; while that other—he who clave to thee,
In mind still unbelieving, yet in heart
Beyond all power of unbelief convinced ;
That weak one, in the heaviest hour made strong
As I am made—brought goodly spices here,
That we might swathe, embalm, and bury thee,
Our Master, out of sight of them that slew ?

And what is left me now, but just to bend
Above this form of thine, and kiss thy face,
And look into thine eyes, and think of all
The lovely deeds of thee, and all thy words
Sweeter than woodland honey-drops, wherewith
Thou in old days wast wont to comfort them,
Thy people, wandering up and down the earth;
And all the goodly promise of bright hours
Closed in thy life; and lay the still, cold limbs
Reverently thus; and smooth the golden hair
Back, with its rippling streams, adown thy neck;
And turn from thee, and screen thy resting-place,
And go hence, sorrowful and sick with fear,
Into the blind, mad throngs of wilful men?

THE CHRIST.

He is not dead but sleepeth—
    Yea, though ye laugh us to scorn,
As the dawn from the darkness upleapeth,
    As the night dashes out into morn,
As the moon cleaveth clouds in her glory,
    As the spring flameth forth into flower,
To his side that your spear has made gory,
    To his arm ye despoiled of its power,

To the head ye have wreathed in derision,
  The feet ye have nailed to the tree,
There will come back the beauty elysian,
  There will come life and fervour, the free
Fair light to the lips, and the splendour
  Of thought to the brow, and the rose
To the palm-smitten cheek, and the tender
  Love smile to the eyes that repose ;
And as soft as a sleeper awaketh
  He will wake from the slumber of death ;
As a sun-litten cloud the wind shaketh
  Blowing clear into flame with its breath,
He will shake out the hair from its bindings,
  As tow that is burning his bands
Break through, and the swathes and the windings
  Rend loose with the might of his hands,
And strong as the sun in his gladness,
  Come forth like a king to his bride,
Our Christ whom ye mocked in your madness,
  Made drunk with the wine of your pride.

There is not a bone of him broken ;—
  There is not a deed of him lost
To his world, or a word he hath spoken
  But God hath uptaken and tost
Far away among tribes, among nations,
  Like seeds whirled about in the fields

When the hurricanes leap from their stations,
　And autumn its winnow-fan wields,
And the year goeth forth like a sower
　To sow for the years that will be—
Sweet grass for the scythes of the mower,
　Sweet herbs for the kine of the lea,
Nut-kernels and pippins of apple,
　And the corn shaken clear of its shells,
And flower-seed to deck and to dapple
　Spring's brow with the blooms and the bells.
And though winter drive wild from the nor'ward,
　And the earth be entombed in the snow,
Though the clods be frost-fettered, and forward
　And backward the keen winds blow—
Will ye hold in the might of the summer?
　Will ye rein the strong steeds of the sun?—
Lo, back come the song-bird and hummer,
　And the rillets are glad as they run,
And the woods with their old summer sighings
　Sway green in the gray of the dawn,
And the breezes with laughter and cryings
　Tread free in the flowers of the lawn,
And the knolls are new-clad, and the mountains
　Arrayed in the garment God weaves
With the hues of the bow of the fountains,
　Of the sun-widowed skies of fair eves.
Will ye cause the cold winter to linger?

Will ye screen in the snows from the heat?
Will ye hold the mad months with a finger?
Will ye trample earth dead with your feet?
Will ye blow back the storms that are blowing,
  Or baffle the tides in career?
Have ye frozen the rivers in flowing?
  Have ye vanquished the Christ with a spear?
Aha! He is back in despite of you!
  Lo ye the prints in His palm!
Reach hither your hands in the might of you;
  Feel ye His side . . . be ye calm . . .
Can a man for his pleasuring smother
  The stars or the sun in eclipse?
It is He, it is Christ, and none other,
  Yea, Christ by the smile on His lips.

He is out as of old in the city,
  He is walking abroad in the street;
He tendeth the poor in His pity,
  The leper that crawls to your feet,
The halt and the maim and the maddened;
  He feedeth the hungry with bread;
He cheereth the heart that is saddened,
  The dying, the loved of the dead;
He restoreth the child to its mother;
  He giveth the wayfarer rest—
It is He, it is Christ and none other,
  Yea, Christ by the love in His breast.

He craveth for virtue and beauty ;
  He cleaveth to good from His youth ;
To witness of truth is a duty,
  Yea, a triumph to die for the truth ;
He toileth from dawn-time till even
  That light may be given to men,
That earth be uplifted to heaven,
  And sin driven down to his den ;
He calleth the meanest His brother,
  He draggeth the tyrant in dole—
It is He, it is Christ and none other,
  Yea, Christ by the might of His soul.

For holiest freedom He yearneth,
  Made blest by the law that is good ;
For justice, clear-eyed, that discerneth,
  Not blindfold in shedding of blood,—
Firm-handed to hold, and fair-sighted
  To watch as the balances sway ;
And for Him is the black heaven lighted
  With streaks of perpetual day ;
And for Him is the world-life a prison,
  By death to be cloven apart—
It is He, it is Christ re-arisen,
  Yea, Christ by the hope in His heart.

His face to the night He uplifteth,
  He searcheth the stars and the sun,

For the secrets they hold ; and He sifteth
   The sands where the gold-rivers run,—
The rivers of knowledge, of wonder,
   That roll to the infinite deeps ;
Hid treasure He draweth from under
   The caves of the hill where it sleeps,
And the waifs of old time that are lying
   Where the earth of dead centuries lies—
It is He, it is Christ the undying,
   Yea, Christ by the thirst in His eyes.

He trampleth the seas in His pleasure ;
   He soweth the desert with flowers ;
He dareth to strive and to measure
   His power with invisible powers ;
He burneth the idols with fire ;
   From the courts of the temples of God
He scourgeth the seller and buyer,
   He driveth them forth with a rod ;
And His sword He hath sheathed, in His craving
   For love in the turbulent lands—
It is He, it is Christ the all-saving,
   Yea, Christ by the strength of His hands.

From the cloud-folded ultimate regions,
   East and west over measureless seas,
Come thronging the myriad legions
   Of the good, of the wise, at His knees

Bowing down, and from hands heavy-laden
  For gifts pouring pearl and fine gold;
Yea, the youth high of heart, and the maiden
  Pure-eyed, and the rulers of old,
All the just, and the great, God-appointed,
  Come thronging with reverent pace—
It is He, it is Christ the Anointed,
  Yea, Christ by God's light on His face.

Ere the world was rolled forth into spaces
  Of light, into regions of day,
Ere the waters ran over dry places,
  And the grasses sprang green from the clay,
His rest was of old with the Highest,
  He abode with the Infinite King,
He was King from the first, and the nighest
  To God, and we praise Him, and sing,
Lifting hands to the throne of His splendour,
  Sing aloud in our joy, ' It is Thou,
It is Thou, O Christ, our defender,
  Our King by the crowns on Thy brow !'

He made Thee a King to reign over us,
  God, who is thronèd on high,
Whose wings soft-shadowing cover us,
  Curved wide as the sky ;
Who is crowned with the suns, O Supernal !
  Who is girdled about with the stars ;

At whose feet the strong oceans eternal
  Are crouched in their bars ;
Whose breastplate is darkness ; who scatters
  The robes from His shoulder like fire ;
Who calleth from chaos and shatters
  The worlds in His ire.

Thou movest a King everlasting,
  Thou abidest with man to the end ;
Thou art with him to comfort him, casting
  Thine arms close about, to befriend
In the moment supreme of his sorrow
  That is blackened with Death for his doom :
For Thou givest him hope of a morrow
  Of rest—we are strong in the gloom,
And we know that the sun going seaward
  Will arise at the morn from the sea,
As we strain from the bow, looking leeward,
  While the wind in our hair bloweth free,
Looking forth at the mountain-tops cleaving
  The clear golden spaces of light,
And we spurn at the shores we are leaving,
  And laugh as we drift into night.

Thou changest from glory to glory,
  Thou growest for man as he grows—
As peak after peak, high and hoary,
  Palm-plumed, clad with vine and with rose,

As bay after bay that with thunder
   Of breaker on cliff and on sand,
Running inward afar, rolling under
   Great capes of a bountiful land,
Bursts full on the voyager sailing
   By coasts of a tropical clime,
In sunlight, in moonlight unveiling,
   Receding, so Thou in our time,
In the days God hath made for our moulding,
   As we fleet on our way, evermore
Enlargest, upheavest, unfolding
   Thy beauty, thy light, and thy power;
And as ever we speed to the ending,
   As earth rolleth on to her goal,
Thou wilt lend us thy strength, ever blending
   Thy light with the light of the soul,
Till to nought hath our labour diminished,
   And the deeds have been done God hath willed,
And the work God hath set man hath finished,
   The purpose of ages fulfilled,
Till the stars from their cycles are shaken,
   The sun from his fervour hath waned,
And Life in our hands we have taken,
   The realms of our glory attained!

THE FALSE CHRISTS.

'And there shall come false Christs.'

Unto three kings the years have given birth,
　Three throned by men, and crowned, the first
　　with gold,
　The second thorns, the third a simple fold
Of stained cerement.　And these hold the earth.

Now, the first king is gorgeously arrayed ;
　Gold is his crown, and golden cloth his robe,
His breastplate gold with myriad gems inlaid ;
　And with his foot he covereth the globe ;
And in his hand he holdeth ready-drawn
　A falchion double-edged, to smite and slay ;
And round about his throne at eve and dawn
Stand mailed men, the weapons of his sway ;
　And he is hard and ruleth cruelly ;
　And at his will must all men bow the knee ;
And for his favour will his servants wear
Sackcloth and ashes, gash themselves with knives,
In flame or torrent fling away their lives ;
　Yet will he not his tyranny forbear,
But sitteth smiling at a race down-trod,
　Wasting his servants with a selfish care,
And craving woes ; and so blasphemeth God.

The second king is like unto the first,
But lowlier; humble are his mien and dress,
Nor doth he in his heart for splendour thirst—
Wearing the guise of pain and long distress :
Yet is he bitter in his ways and cold,
And cutteth off his servants' hands and feet
Lest they should grow in searching overbold,
Lusting that light for which the heart doth beat.
He darkeneth their path with wings of night
Lest in its sheen his servants may delight;
Of the world's best he would not have them
share,
And holdeth clenched in his hands the keys
Of those fair gardens where the bounteous trees
Fruits of free life and of sweet knowledge bear :
He trampleth down the flowerets in the sod,
Cursing their beauty; yea, what God called fair
He calleth foul; and so blasphemeth God. .

And the third king in pride of lowlihead
Is like unto the second : in his pride
His bleeding hands he showeth (having shed
Blood for his servants) and a bleeding side ;
Then doth he point them out a gulf of flame,
Saying, 'My blood hath so appeased His ire
Who sitteth on His throne and is the same
For ever, ye are rescued from that fire ;

Yet if ye seek not to observe my will,
Behold the gulf that gapeth for ye still ;
To save yourselves is of all cares the chief ;
To 'suage His anger I by you am slain '
(This king is weak and wandereth in brain)
' Therefore in *my* great love I crave belief :
Have I not broken the Avenger's rod ? '
Thus teacheth he, and addeth grief on grief,
Darkening God's ways ; and so blasphemeth God.

Such are the three crowned kings in their degrees.
These are False Christs, and we will none of these.

THROUGH THE SOLITUDES.

I.

IT was long past the noon when I pushed back
    my chair
  In the hostel, slung knapsack on shoulder, and
    walked
Through the low narrow room where the folk from
    the fair,
  Old peasants deep-wrinkled, sat clustered and
    talked

D

In their guttural Gaelic; and out through the stalls
  Girt with marketers laughing, and groups here
    and there
Of maidens blue-eyed, hooded figures in shawls
Of scarlet, and wild mountain lads in long hair,
Rude carts, and rough ponies with creels; gaily
    passed
  Up the street; through the starers and bar-
    gainers prest;
And asked of an idler my way; and at last
  Struck out on the hill-road that winds to the
    west.

II.

And I thought, as I strode by the last heavy cart
  Moving earlier home than the rest (wife and child
Sitting close on the trusses of straw, and apart
  On the road, cracking whip, chatting loud,
    laughing wild,
The husband and sire in knee-breeches and shoes),
  Though it was of the first of such journeys to me
Since my life's friend was lost, yet I dared not
    refuse
  The gift of good angels that even, the free
Glad heart in my breast, the delight in my soul,
  As I greeted the hill-tops, and saw down below
The sea winding in from afar, heard the roll

Of the stream on the rocks, felt the autumn air
　blow
Through my hair as I moved with light step on
　the way :
And I said, 'Let me drink to the dregs the
　black çup
Of pain when 'tis nigh ; but if joy come to-day,
　Let me drain the last drop of the demon-wine up.'
Then I journeyed along through the moorlands,
　and crossed
The mad stream by the bridge at the crest of
　the creek,
And wound up the mountain to northward, and lost
All sight of the village and hill-folk.

III.

　　　　　　　　　　A bleak
Heavy cloud, dull and inky, crept over the sun
And blackened the valleys.

IV

　　　　　　　　In under the hills
Ran the road, among moors where the myrtle
　stood dun,
And the heather hung rusted. The voice of the
　rills
Was choked in grey rushes. No footstep was nigh.

One rush-covered hut smoked aloft.   Not a bird
Or a bee flitted by me.   The wind seemed to die
  In the silence and sadness.   No blade of grass
    stirred.
Not a tuft of the bog cotton swayed.   Lone and rude
  Grew the path ; and   the hills, as I moved,
    stood apart,
And opened away to the drear solitude.

v.

Then a sorrow crept writhingly over my heart
And clung there—a viper I dared not fling off.
  The sound of dear voices sang soft in my ear
'To mock me, dear faces came smiling to scoff
  At my loneliness, making the drearness too drear.
Up the track now to right now to left as I clomb,
  Weird visions came thronging in thick on the
    brain,—
Of days long forgotten, of friends, of a home
  By death desolated, of eyes that in vain
Gazed out for a soul that no more would come
    back,
  Of one face far away drawing out my life's love
Very strangely that day to it.
              Everywhere, black,
  Storm-shattered, the mountains loomed lonely
    above.

A horror, a sickness slipt down through my blood.
All my thoughts, all my dreams, all that
memory's load,
All the terror of loneliness, broke like a flood
Over body and soul, and I shrank from the road.

VI.

I cowered at the frown of the mountains that hung
On this side and that; and the brown dreary
waste;
The barren grey rocks far aloft; for they wrung
My soul with dim fears; and I yearned but to
taste
The sweets of companionship, yearned to return
To the far away village; to hear once again
The buzz of kind voices about me; to spurn
The sadness and horror, the fear and the pain.
Then I bent down my head as I moved, and my
mind
Ran out in vague musings:
'If God laid His hand
On my life now, and suddenly, swiftly consigned
My soul, at a breath, to the dim spirit-land—
Guiding on to a world that at best would be
strange,
Would be sad in its joys, in its sweetness
unsweet

To a mind rent away in so awful a change
　From a world of bright faces, the park and the
　　street,
And the room, and the glances of languishing
　eyes,
　The smiles of red lips, and the touch of soft
　　arms,
The gay merry laughters, the happy love sighs—
And I found myself out in a region of storms,
Out beating my way through the waste, with one
　star
　In dark heavens to lead me; through regions
　　unknown,
Dim regions of midnight outstretching afar;
　A bodiless soul on its journey alone :
Ah, methinks I would yearn for a land such as
　this,
　For a cloud that but darkens the *sun*, for the
　　strife
With dim dreams, for the heights that shut out
　the near bliss
Of dear home for a little. . . O life of my life,
My lost one, thou stay of my childhood, my youth,
　Thou fount of my joys in the days that are gone,
Where, where in the darkness, the regions of
　drouth,
　The realm of the dead, art thou journeying on ?

Is it strange to thee now that new being of thine ?
  Dost thou fear in the midst of the darkness, and
    yearn
To be back in the sweet human throngs, in the
    shine
  Of the bird-waking sun, 'mid the soft eyes that
    burn
With love and with bliss ? . . art thou lonely as I ?
  Art thou sad in a world that belieth its God
In its pitiless coldness ? ' . . Then up to the sky
  I lifted my face, and I cried unto God.

VII.

And when back from the dream I had come, every
    rock
  Had a livelier tinge, and the frown from the
    heaven
Had faded, the mountains no more seemed to lock
  My lone life in their folds out of hate, and the
    even
Grew cheery, grew sweet, and a light wind
    upsprung
  'Mid the grasses, and fanned me, and wooed me
    to roam
Through the moorland to seaward, and blissfully
    sung
  In music as soothing as whispers of home.

And at last when the sun had gone down to his
    sleep,
And I caught the Atlantic's loud roar from the
    west,
Saw the flare of the lighthouse, and wound to the
    deep,
All awe of the wilds had died out in my breast.

DITTY.

Come back to days of summer,
    Come back to smiles and trust,
Meet eyes and laugh together,
Bring in the blissful weather,
Gay leaf and glancing feather,
    And fields of flowery dust,
And songs of bird and hummer,
    Lush fruit and honey-crust,
And fear me not nor shun me,
My love whose love's undone me;
Come back to days of summer,
    Come back to smiles and trust.

O love, thou'rt like the dawn-wind
  That sighs across the sea ;
For at its sweet upspringing
Sad dreams will cease from stinging,
And clouds of fire come winging
  From sunward o'er the lea,
And forest-land and lawn find
  A heart for shouts and glee,
And the laughing leaves are shaken,
And night is captive taken—
O love, thou'rt like the dawn-wind
  That steals across the sea.

O love, thou'rt like the flowing
  Of wine on fainting lips ;
For swift there comes a gushing
Through silent veins, a rushing
Of life the pale cheek flushing,
  And, like a star that clips
A path through blackness glowing,
  A light from pallor slips,
And eyes are strong and certain
Beneath their lifted curtain—
O love, thou'rt like the flowing
  Of wine on swooned lips.

O love, thou'rt like the fervour
  Of suns in happy spring,

When flocks of clouds are shifting,
And flights of sea-birds lifting
And like a snow-storm drifting,
    White seabirds grey of wing;
Spring sways, and none may swerve her,
    All joys about her cling,
God's palms are stretched o'er her,
And Death is dead before her—
O love, thou'rt like the fervour
    Of suns in fervid spring.

O love, thou'rt like the breathing
    Of music subtle-sweet;
For all the soul is saddened,
Made faint, and faintly gladdened,
Made wild in mirth, and maddened
    With dreams that flash and fleet,
Made free like white waves seething,
    Made strong like winds that beat
Wide wings in leaves and grasses
With light that broods and passes—
O love, thou'rt like the breathing
    Of music strange and sweet.

Come back to days of summer,
    Come back to smiles and trust;
Lift laughter-lightened faces;
Bring in the leafy mazes;

Bring apple-blooms and daisies ;
  Bring breath of róse, and gust
Of songs from early comer,
  And scents of vine and must ;
And shrink not, fail not, dearest,
And fear not, as thou fearest—
Come back to days of summer,
  Come back to smiles and trust.

———◆———

KISSES.

WHEN I sprang up from a dream last night,
  And kissed, kissed, kissed, across the air,
Where wast thou then, thou darling,
  Where, thou dearest, where ?

I have kissed thee never in life, nor dare,
Yet those pure lips were thine, I swear,
That clung so hard, that cleaved so fast,
That pressed so close—till away they passed,
And I fell back upon the bed,
  With soul full-fed.

A LIFE'S LOVE.

WE met amid the meadowlands
  At dawning of the day,
She to the east and I to the west
  Journeying on our way.

A glance from her eyes, and a smile from her
    lips,
  And the gust of a lovesome song ;
And into the heart of the blissful grove
  She lightly tript along.

But my lone path ran over the hill
  And across the weary plains,
Into the night, and into the storm,
  And into the snows and the rains.

ECHO-SONG.

I.

HA-HA ! aha ! my Echo brave,
Still living in your mountain cave ?
I've journeyed lone since break of morn
By glacier blue and snowy Horn,

Through spectral troops of bearded pine,
Without one voice to answer mine,
Till, singing here my roundelay,
I've caught your cry from hollows grey,
And so I fling my staff aside,
And, ere I pass, whate'er betide,
    Ha-ha ! aha ! my Echo true,
    I'll have a merry hour with you.

II.

Ha-ha ! aha ! my Echo mad,
Must lonely laughter make you glad ?
Must sorrow bring your heart distress
Amid the mountain wilderness ?
Must foot of startled wayfarer
Your cruel wanton mockery stir ?
Must cannon-boom and bugle-note
Find answer from your strained throat ?
And what regrets are yours when lone
You languish on your marble throne ?
    Ha-ha ! aha ! my Echo true,
    Confide to me, as I to you.

III.

Ha-ha ! aha ! my Echo clear,
When Herè bent a charmed ear

To list your voice on noiseless nights,
That tempted from Olympian heights
Old Jove to godless sports of earth,
I ween your speech and warbled mirth,
Your nymphic face and oread-art,
Would cheer her light immortal heart
Not more than, void of nymph array,
You cheer this mortal heart of clay :
    Ha-ha ! aha ! my Echo true,
    Cry glad to me, as I to you.

IV.

Ha-ha ! aha ! my Echo gay,
I've got a bitter word to say ;
The world would laugh my wrongs to death,
But you will hark my mournful breath :—
I've wandered now through half the day
By ferny cave, by torrent-spray,
By leafy wood and castle grim,
By cloven ravine cold and dim,
Yet never form, or eye, or voice
Has awed my breast or bade rejoice,
    Ha-ha ! aha ! my Echo true,
    Till here I heard that note from you.

V.

Ha-ha ! aha ! my Echo good,
They've driven the Dryad from her wood,

They've driven the Naiad from the foam,
The Oreads from their mountain-home ;
There's ne'er a ghost in ghostly tower,
Or giant left with eye to glower,
Loup-garou, ghoul, or banshee dire,
Or dragon fierce with fangs of fire :
They've rid the lawns with deadly swoop
Of nymph and sylph and elfin-troop ;
    Ha-ha ! aha ! my Echo true,
    They've rid the hills of all but you.

VI.

Ha-ha ! aha ! my Echo blest,
'Tis but a meagre joy at best
For days in sacred paths to tread
And find the old delights are dead.
Say, how shall poets vex the brain,
While now the old delights are slain,
Until they find diviner dreams
To throng anew the hills and streams,
Since only empty earth is left,
The soulless wood, the darkened cleft,
    Ha-ha! aha ! my Echo true,
    And all are lost, are lost, but you ?

BABBLE.

Silvery rivulet, merrily murmuring,
What are you talking of, what are you laughing at?
Will you not tell it me, rivulet, rivulet,
Silvery rivulet, mocking me laughingly?
Reason nor rhyme can I read in your murmuring:
Tell me the words that are wed to your melody.
Here on the grass am I waiting and wondering,
Bending to hearken and eagerly questioning,
Wooing your confidence, flattering lavishly,
Like a poor lover entreating his lady-love :
Yet you go mocking me, laughingly mocking me,
Yet you'll not answer me, rivulet, rivulet,
Silvery rivulet, cold-hearted rivulet !

Robin that pipes in the willow-bough over you
Sings a plain melody quite comprehensible ;
Calls to his pretty mate, ' Come to me, come to me ;
Here am I waiting, my pretty one, lonelily ;
Come to me, come to me '—mournfully calling her.
Skylark that warbles above us so cheerily
Talks in a tongue that'll need no interpreter ;
Tells that the nest is all safe in the meadow-grass ;
Tells that the little ones soon'll go wandering

Into the beautiful, beautiful fairy world;
Tells how delicious a flight up to heaven is,
High in the balmy air warbling and fluttering ;
Sweet is the climbing and sweet the return to
    earth,
Diving adown to the nest in the meadow-grass.

Language of breeze and of bird is well known to
    me,—
Why will yours, rivulet, ever be mystical ?
Turbulent rivulet, meaningless rivulet ! . .
On you go mazily winding and wandering ;
Here the sun kisses you, here the rock teases you,
Here in his soft arm the meadow embraces you,
Here falls the tree on your breast and entreatingly
Prays you to pause for a moment and talk to
    him—
I too entreat of you only to talk to me—
On you go heedlessly laughing and mocking us !

Well, then, another day here will I visit you,
Walk with you, talk with you, leap with you, laugh
    with you,
Question you, kneel to you, flatter you, sigh to
    you,
So it may be you will solemnly speak to me,
Tell me the meaning that's hid in your melody.

E

CORAGENE'S TEMPTATION.

" And did I say
The Saint had never known true love, who hurled
To the black wave that maiden of blue eyes
Who followed him through all the world forlorn ?—
The books I've read have taught me otherwise."

Ovoca.

CORAGENE.

WHAT if she come not !—then should I be free
To turn from her for ever, to forget
The passionate earnest eyes, and fair white brow,
And touch of slender fingers thrilling through
My flesh like burning fire. I would kneel down
And pray that such oblivion might be mine,
That all the past might grow more black than
    clouds
That cloak the slender moon in winter storms,
So she might fade from memory, and the soul
That hath forgotten heaven find its God.
O subtle-smiling maiden-lips, sweet eyes
Full of love-languor, full of eager fire
That tempts me from high dreams ; O warm white
    arms
And bosom warmly beating with wild love,

I loathe ye . . . back from me !—for I am pure,
My heart clings fast to God, and I am clean
But for this dread temptation.   When a boy,
A tender child that wandered up and down
Among the groves and meadows, in me grew
High aspirations, love of holiness,
Hatred of evil, and through all my years
Have I with earnest care weeded and cleansed
This garden of my soul.   But now, ay me,
The lamp that led my footsteps groweth dim
In the fierce blaze of this strange love.   No stream
That murmurs in the valley moves me now
To worship with its God-given melody :
The waving woodlands bring to me no joy.
When first I tasted of her love, I seemed
To rise above my narrower ways and grow
Greater in wisdom, as I grew in love :
I said, ' She loves me sister-like, and I,
Lonely, will drink a brother's joy in life,
Through blissful interchange of dreams and
     thought ' . . .
Death, death, not love !   I dream of her soft cheek,
Her rosy lips pouting to meet mine own,
And of her soul the insatiable thirst
That leads her forth to follow on my steps,
And burns on cheek and brow whene'er we meet—
I trust not that swift blood. . . . O would that now

I were borne hence, far into homeless lands,
To live with solitary fasts and prayers,
Purging my spirit of the dross of sin
That clings about it !—If she come to-day,
We shall not meet together any more . . .
Ah !—what is that sweet music on the breeze,
And whose the light step treading through the fern ? . .
Forth from the waving branches of the grove,
Thridding the primrose-tufts with gentle foot,
And singing low a mournful song, she comes.
Circling her brow, the wreath of skyey blue
Binds her brown hair that o'er her shoulder falls,
A sombre stream ; and under lashes black
Moves softly her love-languid violet eye.
But there is sadness o'er her mouth and brows,
A brooding shade of trouble, like a cloud
That darkens all day long the summer hills
While heaven laughs in sunshine, and the smile
That lightens on her lips and in her eyes
Has such a yearning sorrow living in it
As tells of pain deep hidden . . .

CATHLEEN.
                    God be thanked,
My trouble is gone over, and my heart
Has found once more its home.   My Coragene !

CORAGENE.
Sit yonder on the gnarled bough, and tell

Why thus you come so weary, thus so late,
And with so much of sadness in your eyes.

CATHLEEN.

Here let me lay my hand in yours, dear love,
And feel that in the harsh and bitter storm
I have found my one sure haven once again.
Late—late ?—ah, would that I were fleet of foot
As the wild doe that leaps the mountain-brooks,
That I might speed to you as my soul speeds !
Weary and sorrowful ?—weary indeed,
But now not sorrowful, but full of peace,
Full of deep peace, my hand thus laid in yours,
Now that my fear is ended. When the sun
Was gathering up the dew-mist round the hills,
I rose—for they had gone at break of day
To chase the deer across the upland heaths—
I rose, I stole away unseen, and left
The hated house, and took the lonely path
That thrids the meadows in the valley. Ah,
The bliss of entering on the journey, love !
How sweet the breath the meadow-flowers of May
Wafted about me ! and the dreamy hills,
The hanging rocks girt with fresh-foliaged boughs,
The tiny cataracts flashing far aloft
Among the mountain ravines, how they seemed
Instinct with love to bless me as I moved

Among them with unutterable dreams,
Unutterable yearnings, and the storm
Of ravishing expectancy that seemed
As it must suddenly cease in deepest sorrow,
Or break the frail heart with excess of joy !
The mountains narrowed round me, and half-awed,
Yet moving as one seems to move amid
Such strange enchanted regions as the eye
Dreams of when strong tumultuous music breathes,
I entered in beneath the branching woods
That clothed the craggy barriers of the glen.
The morning air amid the myriad leaves,
The still, pure air below the screening boughs,
And down among the blue-bell beds, and plots
Of springy moss, was one soft ringing noise,
Twitter and buzz and warble and low trill
And babble of bright rivulets unseen.
And there I sat me down a little space
Aweary, drinking in the fragrant breath
Of wild flowers and the wandering breeze of morn ;
When suddenly the shouts of mirthful men,
Mingled with many an echo of the rock,
Broke through the ravine ; in affright I rose—
That way the stag had fled from cruel death—
I dared not keep the path, I dared not turn
And seek the open valley : then I plunged
Adown the brake and fled across the woods.

And so I have been wandering up and down
All the long day, seeking whatever path
Might lead to you, dear love, now on the hills,
Now in the wildering woodlands, till at length
God's angel bore me hither—though so late.

CORAGENE.

Cathleen, I had all but prayed, a moment since,
That we might meet no more . . . ay, draw your
    hand
Thus from me, if you will, and flash the fire
Of your wild eyes, reproachful, on my face.
There is a grievous burthen on my heart
That I would fain fling from me. Hearken to me
And earnestly give heed, while now the power
Of Heaven is in me, lending strength to speak.
There was a time, Cathleen, not long ago—
Nay, not so long but that my wounded life
Gapes even now, unhealed, and bleeds anew—
A happy time, ere yet the name of sin
Had lost its bitter flavour on the lips ;
A happy time, for then the light of God
Shone full across my path, and all my heart
Clave unto holiness. I could not roam
In leafy woodlands then with soul unmoved
With fervent thankfulness to Him who clothed
The branches in their glory ; everywhere

All nature seemed uplifting hands of praise.
Ah, then 't was passing sweet to live, and feel
God all about me ; sweet to lie and dream
Of worlds beyond this bounded world ; to gaze
On crimson-streaming clouds amid the blue
Floating far outward, and to draw from them
Into my being thoughts divinely fair,
Deep impulses and yearnings, such as made .
My life a splendour in mine eyes.   O sweet
To pour my whole soul out before its God
In full repentance, sweet to consecrate
My body to His work, and take the pangs
Of toil and self-negation with a smile !
Then came the wildering change.   O blissful days
When the new summer-tide of love upsprung
Within my life, and sleeping nature seemed
To break forth in innumerable flowers ! . .
Cathleen, when first my spirit throbbed with yours
In love's divine awakening, I believed
(Though well I knew how deeply I had fallen)
That, being of the soul, that love of ours
Could yield no soilure . . . hearken to my words,
And shroud your eyes from me a little space . . .
My dream is altogether whirled to earth,
And trails its leaves and blossoms in the mire . . .
Fly from me . . there's a devil in my breast . . .
I am no more that Coragene who feared

Even to lay his lips upon your brow,
Dreading a kiss might taint a love that breathed
From the deep Spirit, to lay hand to hand,
Lest pressure of hand should grow as dear to us
As high soul-commune . . . Fly from me, avoid
     me,
Curse me to death with those sweet lips I love . . .
Or rise and bid me leave you, cast me off
With your own mouth—I dare not go unbidden . .
For I would leave you, I would seek out God,
And burn this poison from my flesh with fasts
And prayer and pain and life-long penitence.

CATHLEEN.

Ah, what a dream is this that vexes you !
Till now hath God not smiled upon our loves ?
Hath he not sealed our wish, and left us free
To love unharmed, unheeded ? . . . Turn and smile,
Turn, darling . . . Will the shadow never leave
Your face, love ? . . . Smile, and say 't is but a
     dream.

CORAGENE.

Back, with your hated hands ! . . .   O God, O
     Christ,
Sustain me now, for I am tempted sore,
Let me not yield, keep ye my purpose firm . . .

Ay ? wilt you tempt me, woman ? . . . Nay, now,
 there,
What need of tears ? I mean not any wrong.

CATHLEEN.

Lo, now, I have been straying all the day
In lonely places, whither maiden's foot
Save mine has never wandered; better far
To have lost myself among the mountain wastes
Than thus to meet the chillness of your eyes,
The terrible darkness of your anger.

CORAGENE.

Child,
I am not angered with *you*, not a whit;
In sooth I know no bitterness to you:
Say but you dare not love me, that my soul
Is loathsome in its blackness in your eyes,
And let me hence to wash away my sin.

CATHLEEN.

Nay, for I know 't is but a dismal doubt
Has made you wild and sorrowful. Nay, love!
But sit beside me here among the flowers.
And I will sing to you a gentle song,
And soothe your o'erwrought mind; and by-and-by
The weary dream will roll away, and leave

Your heavens blue and pure and calm once more ;
Or we shall sit all silent here, and list
The birds' low warbling and the streamlet's sigh ;
And if you will it, I shall speak no word,
But cull the primroses, and bind them up
For pastime.

CORAGENE.

Thus, sweet woman-spider, thus
Weave your soft web about me. .

CATHLEEN.

Coragene,
How have I wronged you ? . . ah my own, my
    king. . .

CORAGENE.

Get hence, nor shape your face into that smile,
That woman's love-smile—placid lips, and cheek
Dimpled, and warm eyes widening—flinging out
The soul abandoned for a man to clasp
Or trample as he lists . . draw back your soul. .
Go hence, take you your own way, I take mine ;
My love is dead—you cannot love me more—
And I am grown aweary of the world—
'Tis time this earthly game of ours had end. . .
Now, slay me with your glance of scorn and pride,
And virtuous calm of forehead and of lip.

CATHLEEN.

I know not what you call an earthly game ;
But if your love for me is dead indeed,
I shall not seek to wake it into life.

CORAGENE.

Woe, woe, it is not dead, it is not dead,
But ah, 'tis grown too sinful sweet.   Great God,
May I not tear the beauteous deadly coils
Off from me here and tread them into dust ? . .
The pure, the pure bright dream comes back even
    now
Like summer breaking forth in autumn days,
Rich in all loveliest colours, wafting out
Gusts of delicious balm.   Ah, get thee hence,
Bright mockery, for every leaf is sere,
The fruit is gathered in, the harvest fields
Have nothing left but stubble and rank weeds,
Rank poison-weeds that choke the dying flowers—
The damps of winter and the nightly frosts
Have blighted the fair land.   Not dead indeed,
But who may call it back to life again,
And it so fast a-dying ?   Kindly eyes,
So filled with sacred scorn, so proudly sad,
Turn, turn ; for though I dare not meet your
    gaze,
I feel that it is on me, and it brands,

It sears, it slays ! . . Ah me, the love divine,
Like a pure bubbling fount of water, springs
Up through the frosty clodded earth again,
And will not rest beneath in any bonds.
Forgive me, Cathleen—dare I say forgive ?
Yea, by your eyes I see my sin forgiven.
Now for a moment, while my pulses beat
To the irresistible music of old days,
Lay your true hands in mine, and let me kiss,
Ay, kiss your lips in earnest, sinless love,
My Cathleen, my one friend, my sole sweet star
Holding God's light reflected tender-pale,
When *His* goes down and leaves me dark, as now.

CATHLEEN.

If I have tempted you from godly deeds,
If I have caused you to break vows, or bent
The green boughs of your grand aspiring life
To trail on earth ignobly, out alas,
May God have mercy on my sinful soul !
Love me no more, look not upon my face,
Let loose my hands lest in them there is death,
Touch not my lips lest there be poison there :
For what availeth love that bears no more
The fruit of holy thought, pure purposes,
Heroic toil, the sacrifice of self ?
Prune it away—it draws the goodly life

Out of the roots that feed it. Go, forget
The tempter, leave me, sin not any more.

CORAGENE.

Forget !—ha, ha ! have I not cried ' forget '
To this tempestuous soul a thousand times,
Only to feel the irrepressible wave
Flung back upon me with regathering might ?
You bid me to forget ! alas, sweet face
And love-deep eyes, when have I yet forgot ?
What earnest prayer begun has run its length
Unbroken by long silences of thought,
Long spaces of deep calm wherein the mind
Brooded upon ye, till the sense of want
Was known no more, and God remembered not ?
What wooded vale, what rocky peak, or hill
Deep-clad in heath, or glimpse of far-off sea,
Bears any meaning now save what is drawn
Out of the memory of this love ? . . Alas,
It is my faith—my life's one helm that drags
What way it listeth, whether tempest blow,
Or summer sleep amid the starry heaven . .
There—let it drift me wheresoe'er it will,
Though I be ruined, though I die accursed !

CATHLEEN.

O talk not thus—the wild and bitter speech
So changes you, dear love, from your true self,

And makes me feel so very lone and drear,
As though no friend I had, as though the face
Of God were hidden from me ! And yet, yet,
What pangs, what agony would I not bear
To comfort you, to shield you from these doubts
That pain you, that so wound you. Ah, my love,
Be comforted—would I not die for you ?
O, if my death could expiate your sin,
If sin it be to love me as you love—
And ah, I will not think that you have sinned—
Then would I see your face no more, and die
In seeing not, and take death's icy kiss
As babes their mother's kisses ere they sleep.

CORAGENE.

Ah God ! when I behold your face as now
So sad, so beautiful, with such a light
Of nobleness and truth in the deep eyes,
And on your lips and brow such firm resolve,
Majestic self-devotion, tranquil love,
What is there left but just to fling myself
Upon your breast, and wind my arms about you,
Lost in wild love, forgetful of all vows ? . .
Dear, sit you here, and let us talk awhile,
Now, ere the sun has floated o'er the hills,
Sit here and let us talk before we part.
Ah lily hand, lie thou upon my knee

With slender fingers spread, yet not too frail
For such a palm as this to smooth adown
That never yet hath wielded any sword ;
Poor pretty hand—ah me, how passing strange
These hands of ours, so full of life in life,
More fearful than dead eyes in death . . Nay, sweet,
Draw it not thus away so suddenly—
What, shuddering ? ah, the early summer winds
Breathe treacherously keen at times . . here, now,
This cloak will cover you full well . . yea, so,
Lie softly thus about the shoulders fair,
And thus about the arms more dainty white
Than whitest roses in sweet-scented June,
And thus about the fairly-rounded waist,
And thus, and thus, about the breast beloved,
The warm true breast, where I in my great pangs
Would fain lay down my head.   And yet, me-
        seems,
In all my care, the warmth of summer glows
In every languid straying gust that wafts
The hawthorn odours up the glen, and shakes
The bells and lingering violets round our feet.
Ah, my dark tresses, flowing down so free,
So glossy-smooth, how have I dreamed of you
A-nights, while ye have made the pillow sweet
For one to dream of me . . is't so, my dove ?
Nay, but I need no answer.   Pretty lips,

Will ye be smiling thus for evermore ?
Laugh, then, for am I not a sorry fool ?
Nay, I will kiss you into rest again.
There, not at peace yet? . . cannot ye be calm?. .
Still smiling ? . . then, one long, long kiss . . alas !
Now are ye sadder than cloud-shadowed woods !
Must I kiss back the laughter and the smiles ?
My Cathleen !—

CATHLEEN.

Nay, I'll laugh without a kiss :
I was but thinking of the strange wild day
When your first kiss upon my cheek, alas,
Seemed so to cling to it, and burn upon it,
That when I met the glance of other eyes,
Fain had I hid my face and passed unseen ;
And when my father drew me to his heart
I dared not meet his look, but hung my head
Abashed, and then he kissed me on the brow,
And like a guilty thing I slipt away,
And felt as though I had stabbed him—strange
    that now
I go home to him proudly. . . Well, but, love,
If *you* look sad, how shall I make you smile ?

CORAGENE.

Press close your lips to mine, love, close and close ;

F

Press close your cheek, and look, love, in mine
    eyes . .
Yea, I can feel the lashes move, yea, see
You love me and will love me to the end.
How can I get, sweet, nearer to your soul ?
If mine arms clasp you, if mine arms are wound
Close round your neck, if my lips cleave to
    yours,
Ah dearest, 'tis to draw you near and near,
Draw you to me that soul may lean on soul,
Even as now. And we have gained indeed
The dearest gift of earth, and vanquished fear
That pushed the soul back in supreme desires
And yearnings.—Speak, love . . . Nay, you would
    not speak ?
Then shall I ask not any word of you,
Knowing you, feeling with your soul, and felt
By yours in very sooth. Ay, better far
This love than any bliss my life hath drunk ·
Under God's sun. Ah, lean thus on my breast,
And let my hand thus wander o'er your hair;
Keep the dear arm so, laid across my neck,
That I may feel its pulses throb.

CATHLEEN.
             O say
You have sinned not, and my sin you have forgiven.

CORAGENE.

Forgiven? nay, I'll crush the bitter word
To death upon your lips. Forgive you?—ah,
Lift up your eyes, and smile upon my face,
Look up, dear love, and know my soul is yours.

CATHLEEN.

Let me begone : the sun is very low :
The way is long : and I would go alone
To-night : let me be going now, dear love.

CORAGENE.

Why do you lay your head thus on my neck
Like one half-swooning, while I press my lips
Only among your tresses? Love, lift up
Your face, and kiss my lips.—Your eyes are
    closed ;
Your lips hang wide.—Sweet love, 'tis best to
    part,
But kiss me once again before you go.
. . . Gone—and I cannot choose but watch her pass
Along the footpath by the torrent's brink,
And swift across the torrent by the rocks,
And up the hill, slow-climbing. How she moves !
O subtle grace of limb, O sweet repose
Of beautiful proud head on rounded throat
And queenly shoulder ! How the hair flows back
Upon the wind ! and ah, she waves her hands

Out wildly now and strangely.   The hill's brow
Snatches her from me, and the floating hair
Follows her down the slope . . . farewell, sweet
    soul !

. . . The calm deep peace of evening on my heart
Lies like God's hand.   The sun has left the
    heavens ;
A faint star peers amid the lingering light ;
The stream grows black beneath me ; and the
    breeze
Of twilight steals adown the rocky slopes,
And rustles through the topmost leaves and dies. . .
I grovel to Thee, Lord, upon the earth :
O God, be merciful, be merciful,
Lay not Thy scourge too heavily upon me ;
Draw back, O God, and leave me with my sin.
Wrap Thyself, Lord, in darkness evermore ;
Let not Thy light shine in upon my soul
To show me my pollution. . . O my soul,
How is it fallen, how is it cut down !
O my pure life, how has corruption spread,
Within it, leaving all a hideous mass
Of rottenness, like an unearthèd corpse !
God, God, cannot I shake the tempter off ?
Wilt Thou not blot away that hovering face
That will not cease to smile upon me thus

Though I should sear my eyes with fire ? . . . Sweet
   face—
For thou *art* sweet—I would not have thee fade,
Thou art so strangely, wonderfully fair.
I feel her last long kiss upon my mouth
Now, even now, and the soft loving arm
Here, on my neck, and touch of finger-tips
Straying about my forehead and my cheek,
And all my brain is burning . . . ah, ah, ah,
Back comes the dire enchantment once again
Dragging me down to hell . . . the lily hands !
How the tongue ever frames sweet words to sting
The satiated soul ! . . . the lily hands
With their soft touches on the cheek and brow !
Why cannot I forget her loveliness,
Not try the old temptation o'er again
To yield with smiling lips . . . and yet, perchance,
This is the olden habit of the brain
Still working, not the newer impulses
Baffled before they can fulfil themselves
In outward act and growth of mind : for how
Can the old ways of thought in a moment change,
And would it not be strange indeed if I,
Whose cheek is glowing with her latest kiss,
Should quite forget the sweetness of her lips,
And the light pressure of encircling arms
When the face lifts in kissing ? . . . Out upon me,

Do I not know what this means? Base, base heart,
Foul hypocritic mouth, preacher of truth
With lying lips, false breaker of pure vows,
Deceiver of the world, who cannot yet,
For all thy crafty wiles, deceive thyself!
What hope for him, who, in his strife with sin,
So cheats himself with fancied nobleness,
That each temptation's triumph stirs his blood
With ill-disguised rejoicings? Can there come
Anything noble, any vigour of heart,
Or earnest self-rebuke from such an one?
I know my nature through—my sense of truth,
My godlike instincts, and the purer dream,
The child's gift to the man ; and close with these
My self-deceiving good thoughts of myself,
Wherewith I deem that I may blind the sight
Of all-beholding God, resting at peace,
With scarce a sigh for Heaven, or fear of Hell.
Yet O to gain Thy ways once more, and breathe
The cool refreshful air of righteousness !
Is it not dearer than this withering love,
This ever-troubling and tumultuous joy,
Or rosy-sweet oblivion? . . . Get thee back
Into eternal night, thou glorious form,
Be thou once more as utterly nought to me
As ere my life was kindled into flame
At thy first dawning . . . yet it *will* not fade—

How all that marvellous beauty shines! white arms,
And womanhood's dear splendour ! O Great Christ,
With what a villain hunger have they cursed
This grovelling life, beating me down to earth
Remorseless, in exultant victory !—
Were this pervading image of the brain
But the true body that one's hands might touch,
Then might one, moved to terrible despair,
Strike a fell stroke, and rid his soul of it ;
But who may crush the vision of the eye
That mocks our anger with perpetual smiles,
Fading, and flashing back, and flashing back,
And clinging to the sight inseparably
As clings the light or darkness ? O my God,
When she is near me I am tempted sore
Into wild ways of passion, but ofttimes
The memory of all that loveliness
Of bodily form, while no rebuking *soul*
Seems breathing in it, lashes me with power
More awful than the hurricane with the boughs
In the tumultuous woodland—every nerve
Quivers within me, and the eager joy
Catches the breath and shudders through the frame,
And I am but a plaything in love's hand,—
Love that exalts not, but is as a storm
Of ravishing sweetness, of delicious pain,
Of fierce, devouring bliss.

Have I not sought
Forgetfulness by many an earnest means ?—
Dwelling apart from her for many days :
Preaching the truth of God to simple souls
That yearn for it amid the ignorant lands ;
Oft folding up my mind in alien thought,
Reading hard books, and dwelling on the words
Of noble hearts forgotten ; or myself
Building great schemes, and showering on the page,
Far into night, my own divinest dreams :
And in the midst of speech, or studious thought,
Or strain of memory, back comes her voice,
And nought is left, but suddenly to cease,
And pore upon the image of her face,
Recall her words and ways, how she has smiled
On such a day, with what a tone her voice
Has fallen in speaking lovingly.   And *now*,
On this last day, when I had risen strong
Above temptation, and my soul was firm
In sin's renunciation, soft she comes
With her coy smiles, her deep and lovesome eyes,
Her scorn of me, her pardon, and her tears,
And flings me back to Hell with her dear love ! . .
Better to strive no longer, better far
To slay my conscience outright at a stroke,
For all is vain, all vain, and I am lost—
A desolate, hopeless, and wreck-ruined man.

POET AND MISTRESS.

He speaks.

THOUGH I know that God in the framing of thee
(Thou strange bright creature He loveth so),
While over thy cheek to flash and to flee
He bade the blood, and the great eyes glow
Sudden with pain and sudden with pride ;
  Set the hair to ripple and roll
In its golden streams on either side
  The pearl-pure brows ; and dowered thy soul
With a dower of manifold changeful thought ;
  Gave thee to move with noiseless feet ;
For diverse daintiest labours wrought
  Thy long white fingers fairily-sweet ;
Formed thy mouth for the pout of fear,
  And the bitter curl of a high disdain ;
Lent thee an artist's eye, an ear
  To revel in music's bliss, and a brain
Swift to learn as the tongue to speak—
  Though I know that God with gifts on gifts
Making thee blest, has made thee weak,
  And thy heart is a thing that slides and shifts,
Finding never by eve or morn
  In the one love-mood an hour's repose,

But flashing from pity to pitiless scorn,
  From love of the lily to love of the rose :
Yet now that thine eyes have looked in mine
  And our souls have kissed in the kiss of the lip,
I swear that never that heart of thine
  Out of my resolute hold shall slip.

For I am a poet, all men say,
  I have writ through nigh a decad of years,
Tragedy, comedy, lyric and lay,
  With my cries I have wrung the world to tears :
I am a poet, a maker of men,
  I have wrought the dream to a thing of truth ;
I have uttered all passions, traced with pen
  Griefs of age and blisses of youth ;
And now I will write no more, but straight
  Turn my wit to a dearer use ;
For hour by hour I will lie in wait,
  And watch thy face, and ponder and muse
What is the thought and what the dream,
  And what the life that accordeth best
With thy mood : then all at once I will seem
  To change as thou changest, come forth drest
Now in despair and now in pride,
  Perchance with pomp of a tyrant king,
Perchance like a lover wooing his bride ;
  And out of my mind's full store will bring

All the fancies rich and rare,
    One after one as a host his wines,
Bidding thee taste of a boundless fare ;
    All the passions my verse enshrines,
All the souls I have put in my plays
    In a trice I will grow to.; now I will frown
With a cynic hate of the world's weak ways ;
    Now I will live a light-heart clown ;
And now a saint with fast-shut mouth
    And eye upturned under drooping lid ;
Then, swift as the wind veers west or south,
    Turn to a reckless worldling, rid
My soul of its truth for an hour or so,
    And laugh and jeer at all things high ;
And last at a breath, as the white clouds grow
    All into flame in a sunset sky,
Back I will come to my own true ways,
    Fling to the wind the guise of art,
Sing as I sang in the olden days,
    Sing in the bliss of an earnest heart,
Sit by thee, talk of the pure and good
    As thou lovest to talk when God in His power
Lifts thee into thy noblest mood.
    And the world may cry to me hour by hour,
' Come, poet, sing to us one more song,'
    May laugh as at one who is simple and weak,
And I will laugh back at the purblind throng,
    Turn in my pride and kiss thy cheek.

For love is better than fame, I hold,
  And to gain one heart in God's wide world
Better than all the wealth of gold
  That ever from earth's rich veins is hurled;
And I, while the years into darkness roll,
  Spurning all else for thy dear sake,
I shall have gained thee, beautiful soul,
  Whom God hath lavished his power to make—
While ever from under my false disguise
  Low with myself I will laugh to see
The love looking out of thy great wide eyes,
  And lighting thy lips as thou watchest me.

She answers.

Must I then lock thy mouth thus with my hands,
Thou babbler, ere thou givest me space to speak?
Hath God then left me with a soul so weak
That, passing through the glories of His lands,
I shall not find one thing to prize till death?
Nay, love, if, moving through His gardens rare,
I pass the tulip opened by the breath
Of dawn, to pluck the rose beside the rill,
'Tis not because the tulip is not fair,
Be sure, but that the rose is fairer still:
And if I find the fairest and the best
I needs shall pause before it, bend my brow,
And give God thanks, and take it to my breast,
And clasp, and bless it, as I bless thee now!

AMONG THE VIPERS.

THEN, let them babble while they list,
    And gulp their fill of lies ;
There's *one* will look into thy face
    With trustful, cloudless eyes ;

And here's a hand to help thee,
    And here's a heart to guide—
My friend, my friend of olden days,
    Come closer to my side.

———◆———

THEY are gone through the dusk, and the laughter
    And prattle grow fainter and die ;
They go to their homes making merry,
    And back to my sorrow go I.

But sweeter to me than all joyance,
    And dearer than laughter and play,
Is to sit thus alone with my sorrow
    While eve on the mountain is grey.

AN AVOWAL.

Sweet, do we wrong one another,
　Being so eager and bold?
Touch of the hand and glance of the eye,
　What may not these unfold?
　What has been left untold?

Love we dared not smother
　Hath spoken in signs full sure—
Language of lip may flatter and lie,
　Wilfully framed to allure,
　In vows not meant to endure:

Face to face cannot dissemble,
　Telling a sycophant's tale.
Yea, by the crimson flush of the brow,
　Yea, by the cheek turned pale,
　Thoughts that in utterance fail,

Hands that unheedingly tremble,
　Eyes that in ecstasy meet,
Minds that each other newly endow,
　Hearts that in agony beat,
　Smiles that are playful and sweet,

We are pledged with scarce an endeavour,
    Even to death, sweet dove ;
I am thine, thou art mine, evermore.
    God on His throne above
    Witness our pledges of love !

Yet is there something to sever,
    Something to keep us aloof,
Yet do our spirits a boon implore,
    Claiming an ampler proof
    Even in love's behoof—

Claiming the dear embraces,
    Kiss of the lips and cheek,
Solace of earnest mutual speech,
    Rendering of trust less weak,
    Telling of truths we seek,

And love that nought effaces,
    Merits full freedom I trow ;
So to draw closer the life of each,
    Sweet, I have spoken it now—
    Here on my bosom speak thou !

A REMONSTRANCE.

Ah dearest, art thou not aweary yet
　Of street and buzzing room and gaudy show,
Of dance and shallow talk, and sickly wit,
And laughter insincere, and eyes unlit
　By feelings deep or earnest ?　Dost thou know
How green the wheat now stands in dewy fields,
　And how the hawthorn hedges in the lanes
　Are whitened into bloom by April's rains,
And every tree its leafy burthen yields ?

Hearest *thou* the blackbirds piping in the dawn,
　'Mid lightest slumber and delicious dreams ?
Say, hast *thou* felt the cool fresh grass o' the lawn
About thy feet awandering when, updrawn
　By the warm sun, the mist of morning gleams
So downy-white in heaven, and the boughs
　Hang dewy-moistened through their clustering
　　leaves,
　While the still air no sigh of sadness heaves
Lest yet the brooding bird it might arouse ?

Ah sweet, the woods are wild with melody,
　The very bees are out among the flowers,

And yesternoon, beneath the sunny sky
I saw indeed my first-seen butterfly
On dappled winglet, fluttering 'tween the showers,
And wished my wish in secret. All the air
    Is heavy with sweet primrose-perfumes, breathed
    From mossy banks with violets inwreathed
And lightened 'neath the furze's ruddy glare.

The mountains are all emerald, gold, and blue,
    So fresh and softly shadowed with stray clouds.
Even where I sit I see the sea's deep hue,
And silvery ships that cut the ripple through
    Slow moving to the south with swelling shrouds.
The daintiest sea-weeds bloom about the rock,
    The wave makes summer music on the sands,
    And the stout fisher, plying toilsome hands,
Flings forth a summer song amid his talk.

Leave thou the city, sweet, to colder souls
    That drink not gladness in the leafy woods,
That joy not for the ripple as it rolls
Along the white sea-beach, that love not knolls
    Of wilding flowers, or mountain solitudes.
Come thou, and wander by the gladsome brooks ;
    Come, breathe the mountain air, and read God's
        love
Revealed in earth beneath and sky above
In language plainer than the text of books.

G

IN THE DANCE.

He.

IT is bliss, it is bliss so to hold thee, my life,
  To keep whirling in time, to keep whirling in
    time
To the violin's titter, the din of the fife,
  To the clash of the cymbals, in tumult sublime,
In the beating of feet, in the waving of hair,
  In the babble and ripple of laughter and sighs,
In the flashing of light, in the fanning of air,
  In the gleaming of arms, in the shining of eyes.

She.

It is bliss, it is bliss to be borne at thy breast
  Through the glimmer of pearl, through the
    glimmer of gold,
And to feel that thou lovest me, lovest me best,
  Our vows have been spoken, our love has been
    told.

He.

I love thee, I love thee, my darling, my queen,
  I will love thee in life, I will love thee to death,
While the sea-spray is white, while the olive is
    green,
  While the lip hath its redness, the body its breath;

And our years shall be ravishing sweet—O divine
As the murmur of music, the scent of the brine,
As the flavours of fruit, as the glory of wine—
Yea, shall they not, darling?

She.

My love, it shall be;
For with thee will the gloom be illumined with
stars,
And a low-laughing wind will upleap from the sea,
To dissever the cloud with violet bars,
And to break up the heaven in islets of blue,
And the peach-tree and rose-bush flame into
flower
Like a flame of the sun at the times of the dew,
And the springs at thy bidding outburst in their
power.

He.

And with thee at my side not a day will run drear
But in clouds of torn fire, amid wells of gold-
green,
Light soft as the turquoise that swoons at your ear;
And the glow, as the night-wind its pinion out-
wafts
Will die not, will blend in the moon, in the sheen
Of a silent aurora outshooting its shafts
Far aloft in the blue; and the bird of the night
In the wood will be warbling and warbling till day;

And the waves evermore will be lapt amid light,
  And the flowers amid light in their languor will
    sway.

She.

I will cleave to thee fast, I will stand at thy side,
  I will lie in thine arms like a bird in its nest.

He.

O lean but thy brow on my shoulder, my bride,
  There is none that will heed how-so-near it is
    pressed ;
As they wheel in the noise and the light of the room,
  The rest they are dead, they are blind to our
    bliss.
Here as we sweep in the canopy's gloom,
  Lift up thy lips for a kiss.
Onward, and onward, my dove, let us speed,
  For loud is the clang of the trumpets clear,
And wildering the note of the flute and the reed.

She.

O love, I can nought of their jubilee hear,
  But only the ring of thy voice in my mind.

He.

O sweet, how the breath of the gardens anear
  Comes borne through the lattice on wings of the
    wind !

She.

O darling, I know not of aught save the glow
  Of thine eyes looking down into mine, and the
    taste
Of thy lips on my lip, and thy murmurings low,
  And the warmth of thine arm lying close on my
    waist.

He.

O soul of my soul, shall our lives not be blest,
  When I hold thee and fold thee so fast to my
    heart,
That thou'lt lie like the shell on the rock in thy rest,
  And angel nor devil shall rend us apart?
And we'll fly to the lands of the palm and the pine,
  Where the eyes of the peoples are wild in their
    love,
And the clusters are purple and black on the vine,
  And the heavens are lurid in splendours above;
And we'll sit in the cool of the branches by day,
  And we'll hide in the leaves from the wrath of
    the noon,
And at night in a bark on the tides of the bay,
  Wander with melodies under the moon,
While the months to eternity laughingly roll,
  And the fervour and fire of the heart is increased,
And the love ever springs in the deeps of the soul
  . . . 'Sdeath, why has the music ceased?

LOVE'S COWARDICE.

Not courage to stop in the street and give
A kindly glance or a kindly word ?
And I that through love of you hope, breathe,
  live,
Have passed like a stranger, unheeded, unheard.
What do you fear, then ?—Friend and foe
Gliding about in the shifting crowd,
What if they knew (as I fain would know)—
What if they whispered it, talked it aloud—
That love had made brave the heart in your breast,
  That love had made stronger a soul not weak,
And meeting the man you loved, you prest
  His hand, spoke to him, and heard him speak ?

 . . . To pass and feel the rippling air,
  Moved by us, kissing the lips, the eyes,
And soul thrill soul, so light, so rare,
  And a gush of sweet joy in the heart uprise !
And then the sorrow, the pang, the shame ;
  The flush of pride that leaps to the face ;
The low-tongued murmurs of mutual blame ;
  The doubts that torture us, render us base ;
The long, long yearning unsatisfied ;
  The quenching of hopes that had flamed anew—

And to you the remorse for a grace denied,
And to me, ah God !—the distrust of you !

Is it kind, is it just, to leave a sting
In a heart that throbs for you ? . . Ah well, well,
What strength can the glance of a moment bring
To nourish a life in its toil ? What spell
Can the flash of a ribbon, lilac or brown,
The gleam of the hair of rippling gold,
The rustle or touch of a silken gown,
The waft of a mantle's velvet fold,
Breathe o'er a soul that is sick to speak
The thought that it lives with, sick to see
The love-light dawn once more on your cheek,
And to work as of old, with a love set free ?

You do your love a grievous wrong
Thus to belie it through shame or fear,
Who have smiled ere this in the midmost throng,
Looked in my eyes, and drawn anear,
And told the truth with your whole free heart
In love's clear language, felt no pain
Nor trembled, nor shrank. Why stand apart
Now, and fling down betwixt us twain
A barrier not to be overpassed
Till many a tear of sorrow be shed,
Till the old love out of our lives is cast
And a new love springs from a love that's dead ?

What need to dread that any should learn
    The priceless truth you hide in your soul?—
You have won what the best have striven to earn,
    And which to lose is life's worst dole.
We have cried to Heav'n with uplifted palms,
        That our love might grow more true, more
        deep ;
Told it all out in its storms and calms ;
        Pray'd for long dreams of it blessing our sleep :
And I ask, what cause for an hour's distress
    In a world by kindred footsteps trod
If sister or brother should hear or guess
    The sweetest thing we have sigh'd to God ?

---◆---

IN THE TEMPEST.

STAND by my side,
    Cleave to me fast
(My love, my bride,
    Who art mine at last)—
Cover thine eyes
    Close in my breast,
Till the thunder dies,
    Till the wind 's at rest.

I have fought, I have won,
   I have trod on the world ;
My task is done,
   My banner is furled.
Hath Christ not spoken,
   Hath God not willed ?—
Our bonds are.broken,
   Our dream 's fulfilled !

———◆———

A PARTING.

'MID music of stringed instruments,
In ravishing music, in the tide
Of young wild life, in soft sea air
That kissed our brows, in perfumes rare
Blown through the southward windows wide,
We spoke, and every word was wove
With love, because our lives were love.

A little while, the dance was o'er:
The seaward doors were wide for heat ;
The stars were mild, the night was sweet,
The gardens crept down to the shore.

Among the palms and cypresses,
Magnolia blooms, and cedar trees,
And marble forms in dusky grove
Glimmering, whiter for the moon,
We walked forth in a mist of love.
We spoke no word, we sighed no sighs,
But in the sight of stars and moon
And the full glory of night skies,
We gazed into each other's eyes.
Then her lids droopt with tear on tear.

" O love, O love," I cried to her,
" I journeyed sunward o'er the sea,
And through the zones of storm and shine,
Until these mountains girdled me ;
And as I traversed waves of light,
And cities old, and passes white,
And down the rivers glided free,
Said, ' Somewhere God doth well enshrine
A spirit in whose eyes all, all
That I have sought of love divine,
And truth, and trust, and tenderness,
Lives, my whole being to enthral ;
And He awaits me in far lands,
By some sweet sea to make her mine,
To lay her hands within my hands,

To crown our longing, and to bless.'
I said it over in my heart
Times upon times, and held it true,
And could not drive the dream apart
That clung to me the sweet spring through.
Now take this kiss upon thy brow ;
Say thou believest, as I vow,
God hath decreed—nor shall deceive—
That we shall meet, and love abide."

" I do believe, I well believe,"
She answered, clinging to my side—
" O mine own life ! Thou shalt not tear
Thy soul away. There is no power
Shall take from me the gladness rare
Which this new love has given for dower,
The crown of bliss it round me wreathes.
All the world hath of good and fair
Is blended with the love I bear.
Thy love amid the roses breathes
That blow in pink sweet fields of flower.
I feel it in the fitful song
Of nightingales that, warbling, throng
Magnolia boughs and tropic trees.
I see it in the stars that flash .
Between the flat and dusky boughs,
Of cedars sighing in the breeze.

I drink it o'er the mountain's brows,
And in the spices of the seas.
I hear it in the silvery splash
Of the white spray on glad blue waves,
That chafe and chime in surfy caves
Below the myrtled promontories.
I see it in the leaves of light
The sun beams through; in bird's blue crest
In gold and scarlet fires of night
Cloud-kindled in the burning west.
When at my window o'er the bay
I sit, and watch the sails at play,
And fishers toiling all the day
Along the steep and stony shore,
A golden mist my sight comes o'er,
A liquid music lulls the sea,
And my heart melts in love of thee.
I walk out in the sun, and seem
To walk the air, as in a dream
When one treads free the white waves' tips
And plumy pines with wingèd feet.
I sit to paint, I sit to sing;
I sing of thee, I paint thy lips.
Thou comest with the sunrise sweet,
Thou comest with the moon's white wing;
At sunset and at moon's decline,
The earth is thine, the heaven is thine."

" I cannot sing one song of thee,"
I cried ; " for all my life doth move
In music and sweet poesy ;
I cannot call thee darling names,
Who claimest but as mine own heart
    claims ;
I cannot ask one word of love,
Or any sign to prove a love ;
My heart is in thy breast with thine,
Thy heart, thy love, thy life are mine.
Out of the sea, or blue sweet heaven,
Whence camest thou, by what thought
    driven ?
Such love as this lives free of harm,
Is ours, to shield us and to save.
Lean here thy face, twine here thine arm,
O love, and give Him thanks who gave."

Over the marble balustrade
We leaned, above the moony sea ;
Beside, a green banana tree
Fluttered his pennants of lithe leaves ;
And leaning palms, with tasseled blooms,
And boughs like giant ostrich-plumes,
Made a dry music in the breeze.
She looked up to the heaven, and said :—

"What if the waters roll amain,
What if the mountains in their snow,
What if the white peaks row on row,
Stand up in wrath betwixt us twain ?
Shall love not live though lips be far,
Hand touch not hand, eye meet not eye ?
Shall hearts grow faint, and fleet hopes fly,
Because a cloud across a star
Rolls lightly in a lingering wind ?
Love lives not on the kiss of lips
Or twine of toying finger-tips.
Believe in love, trust well in God :
Be man, nor fear : for Death is kind ;
The high soul spurns the burial clod,
And light is darkness to the blind."
She cried, " It may be the Dark Will
Shall bear me hence, and far from thee :
Love me, and trust me, love me still ;
I trust thee, love thee, doubt thee not ;
Love on and trust, though black clouds blot
Our paths with shadow, dearest friend ;
Trust me, and fear not, to the end."

I said, " The utter sacrifice
Of self is love's strong panoply.
My trust is in thy steadfast eyes
That speak strong truth and constancy ;

And, though I feel in all this air,
In the tree's stillness, in the sea,
In the blue heaven—everywhere,
A sorrow gathering like a storm,
No ill thing in the end shall be."

Then she unwound her glorious arm.

The white moon, turned upon its back,
No higher than a tall man's height,
Hung clear above the olives white.
There was no sound of stream or tree,
No bark of lonely hound, nor clack
Of tree-frog croaking in the vale,
Nor cicade shrill, nor nightingale;
Only the sharp short ripple flung
Against the beach by the bluff tide.
Half round the dark skies' circle wide,
Deep blue, with throbbing stars thick hung,
The cold white mountains leaned aside,
As if they too were nigh their death.
Then a wind rose with moaning breath,
The last breath of the dying night,
And swayed, and fell upon the deep,
And all my heart sank down in death,
Sank as one drifteth into sleep,
Died with the dream of its despair.
I felt it in the mountains white,
I felt it in the low moon light,

I felt it in the faint night air,
I felt it in the still chill tree,
I felt it in the fretful sea,
I felt it in the cold keen weight
Of ice beneath my bosom prest,
And the deep aching of my breast—
It was all over : and my soul
Blindfold through years on years shall grope
Round the dark earth, with famished hope.

———◆———

A DIFFICULTY.

As in Heaven no hate can be,
  Or scorn that worketh dole,
And my hate of thee and my scorn of thee
  Never can leave my soul,

It followeth sure that one of us twain
  Into the flame must go ;
And since *thy* conscience hath no stain
  And all thy face doth glow

With a greasy gleaming righteousness
  And an archangelic dye,
If either it be, thou wilt confess,
  It cannot but be I ;

So there cometh a question of interest,—
Where were it good to dwell?
Which would the rest consider the best,
Thy Heaven or my Hell?

———◆———

IN THE PASS.

AY, night is coming down once more
    With ruin round my path;
The swollen torrents rave and roar,
    The lake's a foaming bath;
They turn me from the hostel-porch,
    And not a home is nigh,
And wolves within the pinewood lurch,
    And eagles swoop on high;
Dear friends that with me gaily roved
    Have perished, and this morn
The best, the trusted, the beloved,
    Slipt from my side in scorn;
There's danger in the wild, I know,
    And night is thickening fast;
More black the inky vapours grow
    Outswept before the blast;

H

The rain spirts down as here I pause,
And hist, the thunder's crash !
Ho, out of yonder cloud's grim jaws
There leapeth flash on flash !
And echoes round the mountain's crest
Roll forth a wild alarm :
But I'll wrap my cloak about my breast,
And walk into the storm.

IN MEDITATION.

THIS is the picture ?   Then, I take
The free-gift from the free.
' Like ?'—O most like : ' but flattering ?'—no,
Too true for flattery.
That hair is just such doubtful gold,
Those eyes the same blue-grey,
As that which round your forehead falls,
As yours that shift and play ;
That upper lip's faint, prideful curve ;
That full lip's fire and fear ;
That tightened nostril's lurking scorn—
(How pitiless ! how drear !)—
That fair smooth circle of the head ;
That white, unwrinkled brow—

(Just where the woven tresses part,
 A shade, perhaps, too low)—
That languid eyelash ; that pale cheek,
 A trifle straight and thin,
Strong in its coldness, strangely weak
 There sloping towards the chin ;
Those eyelids lightly lined with thought
 But seldom worn with tears ;
And those inexorable curls
 Behind the jewelled ears—
They live—it breathes—your soul is here,
 Ay, madam, clear and plain ;
And gaining from your slender hand
 This image bright, I gain
Indeed your heart's true love ? . . clink ! clash !
 Ah ! there amid my weal
I have cast it from me—thus, thus, thus
 To grind it with my heel.

———◆———

A VALEDICTION.

THEN go—forsake me if thou wilt,
 I ask thee not to stay ;
I would not vex thee with my love,
 Or thwart thee one brief day.

H 2

I have sinned ; there's many a poison-thought
    That works within my breast ;
With such high dreams as good men praise
    My life hath not been blest ;

I have lived long years of doubt and hate,
    And scorn of ways divine,
But Heaven !—my heart is pure as dew
    Beside that heart of thine.

GAIN.

Ay, sooth thy sin hath saved me years
    Of bitterest blight and shame,
Thy stainèd honour left indeed
    With me a stainless name.

What is the triumph, what the bliss,
    And what the gain to me ?—
I who had held it honour's crown
    Just to have died for thee !

A RETROSPECT.

COME, let us live the old love o'er again.
Bend near, till I have leaned a little while
My head upon thy shoulder : bend to me
Thy brows for love, and let thy great eyes rain
Their blue beams on my face : and frown, and
   smile
As at my boyish pleadings, womanly—
Mine all-wise goddess of the wondrous brain,
O beautiful in love and in disdain,
My glory, and my gladness, and my pain !—
And be once more all, all that thou wert wont
   to be.

Look back, and count the dark years gliding dim—
Ten shadows, journeying into the void night !
The furthest in their line was a young king
Gold-helmeted, and strong of soul and limb,
To sway wild-willed and glad, when I was ware
First of love's presence as a living thing.
Ten years have turned ten shadows while it
   grew,
Put forth great leaves, and drank the sun and dew,

Flowered, and bore fruit, for blight, and faded
    through,
Frost-folded in the clods whence wildly it did
    spring.

I was a boy, and thou a woman grown :
What marvel that I drank my love's disdain,
Too over-bold in passion for thy pride ?
Yet thou hast said thou lovedst ; and I have known
More in thy warm wide eyes than pity's bane,
When I drew near and nearer to thy side,
When our hands folded flower-like, when thy hair
Fell, kindling neck and cheek and forehead bare,
When I upraised my face with a boy's prayer
To kiss thy proud ripe lips, and was not all denied.

There is no thing in life more tender-fair
Than boy's love for a woman. This thy pride
Played with a season. Then thy wrath arose,
Seeing thyself caught in so poor a snare.
Then fled I wounded to the deserts wide.
The mountain-promontories claspt me close ;
The white gates of the valleys heaved in air
Took me within them ; onward did I fare,
Till my lone life the labouring billows bare
To lands wherein I won that Fame which round me
    glows.

Spread here thy long white fingers o'er my palm :
Still are they smoother than clear ivory—
Yet thinner than of old time, when my lips
Pressed them in fear, and drew in breaths of balm
In kissing them . . How I remember thee,
And all of thine ! ay, to the rosy tips,
These hands ; ay, every little vein that rays
Out from the wrist in blue and wandering ways,
And every delicate line of branching sprays
That down their hollows, curved in myrtly white-
     ness, dips.

And thy hair's ripples ! Let it fall, a space,
And touch my cheek ; yea, let my hands anew
Wander amid its gold, and I will make
A sunset-mist of it about my face.
It grows not now so lustrous as it grew,
Nor in such clouds of glory canst thou shake
Its floods loose. Here's a little streak of grey
Along thy temples. Grief and thought, men say,
Make gold hair silvery. We twain in our day,
Lady, have known of these. Behold the hurt we
     take !

I deemed thy face the sweetest mystery
Drawn to mine eyes from all sweet things of earth ;
Sang of it, limned it, or in marble planned

Clear brows, and lips, and chin, curved delicately;
Learned all its moods of mourning and of mirth,
To count them over. How I cursed my hand
That would not compass in the carven clay
Passion, or pride, or fear, or thy soul's play!
Ah, there's more sadness here than pride, to-day!
Our lives have not run gently, friend, in any land.

But thy scorn's fruit. Have they not sung my deeds
Through the wide lands, and called me king of men?
Thy love was the first rock whereon I stood,
Climbing the vasty heights, in my soul's needs;
Thy scorn the second. O renew again
The ancient commune, yet in wiser mood!
Take of the might thou madest. Lean on me,
Dear sister—friend! Let the dead fancies flee!
Shall not our loves rise godlike, being free,
Of all the fretful griefs and fevers of the blood?

———◆———

A JILT.

ONCE in lovesome mood he said,
    'Ah love, thy face is fair,
Pure thine eyes, and sweet thy mien,
    And bright thy golden hair.'

In a month or twain away she slipt
  Into the throngs of men :
'A loftier lover I'll bring,' thought she,
  'When I come back again :

'My face is fair, and bright my hair,
  And sweet and pure mine eyes ;
Haply, then, in a world of men
  They'll gain me a goodly prize.'

To and fro in the world she went—
  She followed the clink of gold—
Lavishing smiles and weaving wiles,
  And showering glances bold.

One drew nigh and kissed her mouth,
  And half a playful hour
Sucked love-honey, and flitted away,
  To sip from a fuller flower.

And one came buzzing down, of bees
  And wasps and flies a lord,
Lit for a moment at her side,
  And boomèd across the sward.

Then moths with wings of gold and blue,
  Brushing her light dust off,
Went whirling round in circlets gay,
  And made of her life a scoff.

She is drooping, drooping hour by hour,
  And the fresh young life is fled :
None will come to woo her now,
  For none will care to wed;

And if back she fly to the one true friend
  And lover of olden days,
Grovel before his feet in the dust,
  And curse her faithless ways,

What will be laid on him to do,
  Finding her his once more ?
Shall he make her a wife, a mother of souls—
  Or spurn her from his door ?

AT THE DESK.

(A DEDICATION.)

SINCE all the woe, and all the wrong
  These passionate lays enshrine,
In one long bitter tide have rolled
  From that one crime of thine,
I fling to thee what praise they'll earn,
  What curse, what blame they'll win,
And dedicate my life's whole fruit
  To the memory of thy sin.

TRAPT.

But what were you dreaming of, poor little bird,
　When I trapt you and caged you all at a breath?
You lay so still not a down was stirred.
　Was it fear of love, or terror of death?

I had baited my trap for none like you,
　Nay, but for men and the praise of men,
And lay hard by in the grass and dew,
　A panther crouched in a lonely den,

When down you came in a sudden flight,
　You coy bright thing with the mischievous eye;
Poised your head to left and to right,
　And peeped and cheeped and strutted nigh.

I knew your tribe and its tricks and ways,
　For you come to us flaunting bright blue wings,
And curving sheeny necks for praise,
　You beautiful, paltry, traitorous things,

And hover about us, and snare our loves,
　And draw us away in a wild pursuit,
Through thicket and thorn and tangled groves,
　The lair of the lizard, the slime of the newt;

And we hold you never nor win your hearts;
　For ye have no love for a lover's delight,
But vain dead souls full of loveless arts,
　And claws that scratch like a cat's for spite.

So I watched you half in disdain, and smiled,
　Nor cared to have you nor cared to lose—
Let her rest or go; the eyes are mild,
　But it is not a bird for a man to choose.

And there you stay'd, and peer'd and spied,
　And drew anear and anear, and stopt,
Like a weak starved thing in the winter-tide
　Seeking its food, and lightly hopt

Right to the snares in your sight outspread,
　And sprang, and stood inside at last:
Then a sudden resolve shot into my head—
　I drew my strings and I made you fast.

For now that I hold you mine in sooth,
　My cageling caught by my noblest lures,
You shall be my slave in deed and truth;
　You shall serve my will while the freak endures;

You shall come as I call; you shall perch and stand
　On my finger's tip, and peck your grain
One by one from your master's hand;
　Your claws I'll clip that they give no pain;

You shall pipe the set tune I whistle for you ;
    You shall give no sound till I bid you sing ;
And flaunt never more—for I 'll cut clean through
    The bright blue feathers that fringe your wing !

———◆———

A MISGIVING.

YOUR mother was false to her lord, they say,
    When you were a babe at the breast,
Plucked sudden darkness over his day,
    To his heart a snake's fang prest :

She was kissing his cheek one morn, they aver,
    Both arms his neck about,
While she watched her Gallant beckoning her
    From the shrubbery-walks without :

In half an hour she had fled and gone,
    With her smiles and light love-lures . . .
I marvel if your mother, madam,
    Had just that face of yours ?

LOVE-LABOUR.

THEN, go I out at once, love, to the fight :
Since God through that deep craving of our souls
Hath spoken, and I read in thine eyes' light
Trust in this love of mine, and in His might
Sweet faith, I fear not how the battle rolls,
But step forth, dauntless, in love's armour dight.

For, in a brief space back I come once more,
Laden with spoil of conquest,—ivory,
Pearl, gems, and gold—and, entering at thy door,
Down at thy feet my whole rich burthen pour,
And claim thee wife, and crown and honour thee,.
Finding life blest upon this beaten shore.

Else I fall slain ; and then—I feel, I know—
Our God-awakened yearnings, dying not,
In the free gardens of our God shall grow
Fulfilled, and life will need no more this woe
Of battle to keep ours. Behold our lot.
Now, darling, kiss me once more, and I go.

TURBIA.

TURBIA, with what marvel have I seen
How many a time from far thy turret grey
Riving the sun's red eye of blinding sheen
In golden realms of the down-hurrying day !
Strong as the stubborn headland on whose neck
Thou standest, thou wilt still endure, and brave
Sunrise and sunset, storm and battle-wreck.
Yea, o'er the eastern and the western wave,·
Rome's symbol, thou abidest : and old Rome
Abides ; nor shall the blows of buffeting years
Or thee or her annihilate : her home
Is in our midst, thine on yon mount uprears :
Thou with the living rocks thy strength dost blend :
She, with the world's growth, groweth to the end.

———◆———

REJECTED OF MEN.

WHERE in hot winds the heavy curtain swung
    Under a vast cathedral-porch, I saw
One crouched beneath a carven Christ·that hung
Clear from the marble tympan ; mournful eyes
        He had, and with low cries   .
He stretched his trembling hands in vain, to draw

Pity and help from priest and worshipper
That in and out the portal for long prayer
     Went alway to and fro :
' O, for His sake who hangs above your head,
A little water and a little bread !
Ye priests of Christ and callers on His name,
     Help me in bitter need and extreme woe,
          And miserable shame.'
But the good priests did spit upon his face,
And they that went to kneel in that high place
     Shrunk from his rags, with crucifix hand,
And many a lewd one gibed his lazar sores ;
     Till, last, some robèd hierarchs of the land,
     Fierce, angered, breaking from their righteous
          band,
          Down drove him from the doors.
And I, afar off following bitterly,
     Beheld him move with bruisèd feet, sad, slow,
O'er the rude pavements, on by monastery
And palace-doors, by fanes of loveliest mould,
          Pure shrines of jewelled gold,
     Still haunts of learned minds, rich stalls arow
Glittering with merchandise, thro' noise and dust,
In glare of violent noon, a lone man, thrust
          This way and that, and spurned,
And greeted as he went with laughters loud,
Sneered at and hooted by the hustling crowd,
Nigh trodden by proud horsemen, or by wheel

Of gilded chariot crushed ; till, last, he turned,
    And out in pain did reel
Between the soldiers at the city-wall ;
And, issuing by the gates, I saw him fall
    Down underneath the bastions with a groan ;
Then, drawing near, with sickened heart, low bent
    Hard by, and raised his shoulder to mine own,
    And long time watched him, gazing there, alone,
        On that strange face intent.
But while in wonder thus without a word
    I looked into his eyes, about my heart
Crept a strange awe, cold as a piercing sword,
    Seeing in what vile sort so fair a soul
        Had fallen, and what dole.
And suddenly in sad speech his lips did part :
' Lo, all have bowed to devils, drinking lies ;
The fool hath wrought them gods, and the vain wise
        Forgotten wisdom true ;
They see not what they worship, in their pride ;
Not mine but theirs the purpose they deride ;
When truth is in their midst they tread it low,
    Part cherishing dead lies, part lusting new ;
        They know not as I know.'
And when I turned in fear to look again,
His palms were streaming blood, and crimson rain
    Ran from his brows .. 'Ah Lord, come nigh to me !
My Lord,' I cried, 'and have they wronged Thee
    thus ?

I

So mocked, so clothed Thee ?   O, in Thine eyes
  I see
Wisdom beyond all wisdom, and with Thee
  Abide, as Thou with us ! '

———◆———

THE WORLD.

In the black night and on the lonely deep
I saw go rocking in the sleety blasts
The helmless Hulk, adrift, with broken masts,
And naked ribs, and chains that clanked a-swinging:
And through the billows that did round it leap
And clapping of the tempest's gaunt loud hands,
From the hid hold and its imprisoned bands,
Heard, issuing by port and hatch and slit,
Sound of men wailing and a weary singing,
Moan as of prayer or praise that held no hope in it,
But rose and fell away, as rose and fell
The Hulk's lashed stem and stern, larboard and
  starboard side,
While its bell, hanging at the bows unstrung,
Its iron tongue by the heaving swung,
Sent through the noises momently a knell.
So all went by upon the shoreless tide,
Under the night's wings wide.

CAN the cankered bud blow ?
Can the dead come to life ?
Can time backward flow ?
Canst thou be my *wife ?*

Thou art lost, thou art slain,
As a corpse thou art cold.
May God pity us twain !
May *He* love as of old !

A YOUNG FUGITIVE.

'TWILL be a lonely journey : no, not so,
Not so ; it will be sweet to feel that never
We shall part more.   But oh, 'tis sad to leave
All that I love in Padua : my kinsfolk
Will grieve for me : not long, methinks : ah well,
But they will grieve—heigho !   Now, if my father
And my dear mother lived, would I thus fly
To Ludovic?—'tis too, too sad to think on :
Yes, I might leave them to be made a bride,
And they would weep some tears, and then grow gay
Anon : and even so my kinsfolk will :
Then, I shall not keep thinking of it more.

I 2.

I must needs bind this hair up : see how thick
It falls about me : which way best to bind it ?
Thus ?—'tis too clumsy : nay, I'll roll it close
Like a ball—so ; nay, that is not it neither :
Methinks I'll cut it off and fling't away
Into the river—what would Ludovic
Think of me then ?—I'll tie it in a knot
Twisted and coiled thus : well, is that well, now ?
Now must I shape my mouth aright, that men
May deem me a true pilgrim—ha, ha, ha ! . .
Nay, child, you must not laugh so ; pilgrim maids
Smile never . . there 'tis—down at either end—
O you're a very pilgrim.

                                    Where's your staff?
O me, where is my staff, my staff . . here . . no . .
Ah, there 'tis by the window.   O indeed
'Tis very sad to fly away thus : who
Will sit beside my window now ?   Will any
Dream my sweet dreams here, gazing out at night
On the olue starlit heaven ? . . if Ludovic
Should come . . ha, Ludovic will come not here,
Be sure of that, my little maid : I go
To Ludovic—yes, love, I come, I come.

I think I may try now : ah, there are voices
Down at the doorway : hist!—gone now again :
All silent.   I may venture now : poor pilgrim,

God keep me safe from hurt!—Goodbye, sweet
  room,
Goodbye, you dear old window—goodbye, all;
I'll never see you more: but I care not:
I'll not weep after them : nay, that I will not:
Indeed now not a tear: tush, little fool!

———◆———

GAINED IN LOSING.

THOU hast left me strong, in thy sin ;
  In thy pride thou hast left me proud ;
Thou hast dower'd my being within
  With favour above the crowd ;
With memories fresh as the morn,
  With doubts that are dim as the night,
With treasure of love and of scorn,
  With treasure of bloom and of blight,
With dreams from a mind that was great,
  With gleams from a soul that is cursed,
With flashes of hope and of hate,
  With a heart for its God athirst,
With a loathing of love-lit smiles,
  With contempt of the sighs of a maid,
With disdain of womanly wiles,
  With joy in the low dust laid,

With pangs at the dawn and even,
    With griefs for a broken spell,
With a sweet foretasting of Heaven,
    A rich foreknowledge of Hell.

IN THE STUDIO.

LITTLE maid, little maid,
    My bliss and my blight,
Why *will* you keep hovering
    Thus in my sight
By gloom and by glimmer,
    By noon and by night?
Fly away, fly away—
    I am lost in my art,
I can paint but one saint
    (Ah light of my heart!)—
Were it fair if the hair
    Of an angel were curled?
Eh, what would they say,
    The world, the world,
If Madonna should laugh,
    And the Magdalen's cheek
Be dimpled and pink
    Like yours when you speak,

And the little winged cherubs
　Have mischievous eyes
As they swoop in a troop
　Through the violet skies,
And the red beard of Judas
　Hang down at its ease
From tiny rose lips
　Such as these, such as these,
And every nymph's mouth
　Be as tempting as this ?
Kiss, love, and begone :
　Nay, come back, love, and kiss !

———◆———

A LOVE'S LOSS.

I HAD a friend, of women whom I knew
　The noblest—that is scarce a month ago—
And it was sweet to speak with her, and grow
Closer in friendship as time onward flew ;
　And she had known high thoughts and golden
　　dreams,
Strayed where I too had wandered, in lone ways
　Wherethrough the mind goes journeying, drunk
　　from streams

That oft had quenched my thirst on weary days,
And learned to praise the most what most I loved
   to praise.

And I grew proud in trusting I indeed
   Might call her ' friend ' through many years
     to come,
   ' For friends were few enough in life, and some—
Ay, most—could give but little that we need ;
   But diverse notes that harmonize with one,
Two billows bounding shoreward from the main,
   Two rills that through the selfsame valley run,
Could move not more together than we twain : '
I sought her friendship, then, nor seemed to seek
   in vain.

Whene'er we talked together, I would drink
   Her words in wonder, watch her earnest eyes
   Dilate, the tender passionate flush uprise
In her fair face, and smilingly would think
   How great and true she was, in such a mood
How grandly beautiful ; and wish her well ;
   And marvel that no man's soul, strong and
     good,
Had drawn her life to it, nor yet love's spell
Had changed her with that change of which her
   poets tell.

But once, while thus I mused, her eyes met mine,
And downward looked in doubt, then once again
Met mine, with more of softness, more of pain ;
And I who watched her thought, ' my soul and
thine
In love, wild love, could never meet, and I
Am all unworthy of thee'; and that night
We parted as of old : but why, O why
Did her eyes, gazing thus so sad, so bright,
Thrill, through the long dark hours, my life with
such fierce might ?

How have we come to love each other so,
Thou dearest ?—How the world's renewed
to me !
With how much larger hope, with heart how free
Live I and work I now ! A month ago
I was a weak thing, living without aim,
And now there is no deed I would not dare,
To clothe myself with honour, win bright fame,
Snatch from the spoil of the world a victor's
share,
That through my life thine own might grow more
blest and fair.

And yet, in clasping what I dreamed not of,
I have let slip what I had longed for most :

For where is she whose friendship was my
  boast?
Yea, I have lost sweet friendship, gained sweet
  love.
I find *her* not, though seeking near and far:
Fled is the face that gave me joy of yore,
  Gone, like a trackless ever-wandering star:
A new soul's here, but *she* will come no more,
Passed like the dear ones dead unto the unknown
  shore.

WORK-SONG.

Who murmurs that his heart is sick
  With toil from day to day,
That brows are wrinkled ere their time,
  And locks of youth are grey?
'Twas not in such a craven mood
  Our fathers won the lands,
But by the might of toiling brain,
  The stroke of resolute hands:
    For hard work is strength, boy;
      And, whether in house or field,
    Ho! for the men that mind and arm
      In righteous labour wield!

If trouble clings about thy path,
  Ere yet thy days are old ;
If dear friends sink in death, and leave
  Thy world all void and cold ;
Wilt thou lie down in aimless woe
  And waste thy life away ?
Nay, grieving's but a sluggish game
  That coward spirits play ;
    But hard work is strength, boy,
      And when the stout heart bleeds,
    There's ne'er a balm that heals it
      Like the doing of great deeds.

Ah !—lovest thou a bonnie lass ?
  Then, scorn to dream and sigh,
For true love's fruits are noble acts,
  And fruitless love must die ;
And if thy fervency be spurned,
  Go, set to work again—
'Twill help to quench the burning woe,
  To ease the bitter pain ;
    For hard work is strength, boy,
      Whatever the fiend may say,
    And after storm and cloud and rain
      Comes up the cheerier day.

And is a true, true wife thine own ?—
  Let never a murmur rise

To draw one doubt across her brow,
  Or a tear into her eyes :
And if thy children round her knees
  Look up and cry for bread,
O kiss their fears away, and turn
  And work with heart and head ;
    For hard work is strength, boy,
      And with the setting sun
    Come dearer peace and sweeter rest
      The more of it that's done.

And if thou have nor child, nor wife,
  Nor bosom friend, what then ?
Toil on with might through day, through night,
  To help thy fellow men ;
And though thou earn but little thanks,
  Forbear to fret and pine ;
There's One that drank of deadlier woes,
  And holds thee dear for thine :
    And hard work is strength, boy,
      And love is the end of life,
    Music that fires the blood of the brave
      In the midst of battle and strife.

And when thy power is ebbed and gone,
  Lay down thy head to rest,
And the great God will stretch His hands,
  And draw thee to His breast :

Nay, talk no more of sickening heart,
Grey hairs or wrinkled brow ;
Up, up, and gird thy loins for toil ;
    There's good to do enow;
    And hard work is strength, boy,
        And life's a rapture still
    That loses no whit of its joyousness
        To the men of unwavering will.

———◆———

ST. ANDRIAN IN THE ROCK.

Ay me, the little chapel in the rocky banks of Seine,
Rudely hewn by hands that mouldering for many
    a year have lain,
With its poor neglected altar and its pictures
    blurred and dim,
Where seldom rolls the solemn chant or swells
    the joyful hymn.

We came along the river beneath the orchard trees,
And round us lightly floated snow and blossoms in
    the breeze,
The snow like blossoms falling and the blossoms
    like the snow,
While through the April woodlands the birds were
    warbling low.

We entered in unheeded, and all at once his
    voice
Rolled out in mournful cadence, and to me was
    left no choice
But just to fling the deep notes in, while weird and
    wild the chant
Rang round the rocky walls like wail of weary
    suppliant.

Ah, silent is that voice to-day, and all that's left
    with me
Is the life that with the nobler life made blissful
    harmony.
What use is my low strain where breathes no
    melody sublime ?
A broken sheath that hath no sword, a word that
    hath no rhyme.

———◆———

A DAY'S BLISS.

BEAUTIFUL face, how comest thou here
    With timorous eye and earnest smile,
Stirring the blood with blithesome cheer,
    And quelling all pain for a little while ?

Art thou brought from the world to me,
    Or born of the mystic inward mind,
Or a memory, o'er the troubled sea
    Wafted back by a wanton wind?

(Eyes of violet softly fringed,
    Dusk hair rippling left and right,
And cheek with delicate rose-light tinged,
    And pensive brows of virgin white !)

Ah! to-day my heart is high;
    Sweet flowers breathe their life in the breeze;
Airs from under the fathomless sky
    Flutter and laugh in the leafy trees;

With gladsome song the rivulets run;
    Music of birds is awake in the groves;
Meadows toss in a kindly sun;
    White waves dance in the grey sea-coves;

And eyes of men have less of sin
    Lurking under the brows of care;
And noise of toil is a cheerier din;
    And the ways of life are pleasant and fair!

Go not hence, O beautiful face;
    Live thou still in my lonely soul:
Little is here of love or grace,
    Little is here but care and dole:

Smile thou thus, nor fade away,
  Stirring the life with blithesome cheer
Light and peace are mine to-day:
  Let not the dawn of the morrow be drear!

———◆———

A FALLEN LIFE.

I WOULD that the winter were back,
  With the snow and the wind and the rain ;
With its fierce denials of God in the black
  Clouds that stifle and stain
The sun and the sky; with dearth
  And famine abroad in the world,
And doubt and dread at the hearth,
  And death out of darkness hurled ;

That the summer that 's come were gone—
  Ay, never had dawned—and the sun
Never had broken the fog, or shone
  On the ice-bound streams that run
Giddy and glad to-day,
  And the flowers were hid in the sleet
I prayed might dwindle away
  For the coming of health and heat:

For then did our loves upspring,
  And her eyes were earnest and true,
And a sudden word or a look could bring
  A flush to her cheek, and we grew
Nobler each through each,
  And pure of heart, and rose
Closer to God in our speech,
  In despite of the rains and snows :

And now with the roses of June,
  And the blowing gardens, and seas
Calm under sun and stars and moon,
  And laughter in ripples and trees,
And bliss with man and with child,
  And love let loose in the air—
When her eyes are merry and mild,
  And her face tenfold more fair—

She is changed, and is false and bold,
  And smiles to the base with the sweet
Love-smile I had deemed mine only of old,
  Mine when our lives would meet,
Soul with soul in the gaze
  Of our eyes and the clasp of our hands,
In the sorrowful sunless days,
  When pain was rife in the lands.

K

I would I were drowned in the deep,
  Or burnt to dust in the flame,
If only her eyes for an hour might weep,
  And sorrow come, and shame ;
And her false, false heart, with fears
  Smitten, break like a clod
That is bruised, made meek through her tears,
  Thinking of death and of God !

O God, that the light and bliss
  Were gone, and I sat 'mid the roar
Of wintry storms in the boughs, and the hiss
  Of hail at lattice and door,
With her who made misery light,
  With her who made suffering blest,
Ere I found her fickle and slight,
  And the love was accurst in her breast !

———◆———

EN VOYAGE.

I'VE met you east and met you west,
  By sands of breathing seas,
  By groves of odorous trees,
Aloft on mountain's breast,

By dales of pine, by leas
Hung high in Alpine hollow;
    You seem to track my feet,
And I your feet to follow,
    By bridle-path and street,
By carven cloisters olden,
By regal gallery golden,
Two eyes by twain beholden,
    As round the world we fleet ;
And yet we dare not speak, but shun
    All save the glance that lightens
In—friendship, is it, little one,
    Across the face that brightens ?

And must it bear you hence to-day,
    The skiff with shining oar,
    Along the mountain shore,
And far and far away ?
    And I shall lose once more,
Alone and sorrow-laden
    And under alien skies,
My little English maiden,
    Her lips and laughing eyes,
And look that love confesses,
And brown abandoned tresses,
And sunny smile that blesses
    The heart that in me dies

(Alack!) to see the ripple blue
    About the shallop breaking
That bears you hence to regions new,
    The olive-lands forsaking.

I've pushed aside the tendril-twines
    That hid me in their shade
    Lest joy should die betrayed—
I've pushed aside the vines,
    And peering half-dismayed
Above the lake enfolding
    All hues of earth and air,
I scan you unbeholding
    And watch you unaware ;
O bliss, to breathe anear you!
O light, to see and hear you!
O blight, that I should fear you
    Nor once my bliss declare,
Nor press your hand, nor sigh adieu
    Before the mountains sever
Your path from mine and me from you,
    Ah, shall it be for ever ?

And whither, whither speeds she now ?
    And shall I straight pursue,
    Across the waters blue,
With sail and prattling prow

Or stroke of oarsmen true,
And wander where she wendeth,
By lake, or lawn, or bay,
Or wood, or stream that rendeth
The splintered rocks away ?—
Farewell, farewell a season !
To follow now were treason ;
I'll trust in spite of reason
There'll come indeed a day
That I may hold your hand and tell
How chilled of heart you left me
When those light sails that nor'ward swell
Of two brown eyes bereft me.

Ah, where will that day dawn for me ?
In tracts of northern ice,
In lands of myrrh and spice,
By stream or wold or sea—
Or field of Paradise ?
Will death come first or after ?
Will hair be dusk or white ?
Will tears be sweet, or laughter ?
Will love be wrong or right ?
Will you be maid or mother ?
Shall I be lord or brother ?
Shall we be one another
At all, or other quite ?

Will morning breaking blue and gay
  Bring in an age of sorrow ?—
Or will our paths that part to-day
  Unite again to-morrow ?

———◆———

SUMMER RHYME.

LEAF on the bough and fly on the wing,
Birds that sing, winds that swing
Roses thickly clustering,
Woodbine-blooms that clamber and cling,
Ferns that fresh in the woodland spring,
Flowers that sweets to the breezes fling,
Babble of streams and drip of wells,
Golden gleams and balmy smells,
Bees a-buzz in odorous bells,—
What is the word their gladness tells,
  What the bliss they bring ?

Summer is loose and Spring's away ;
Hearts be gay ; pipe and play,
Revel and laugh the livelong day,
Bind the brow with bloom o' the May,
Lave the limbs i' the foam and spray,
Whirl i' the dance at evening grey,

Beat the moss with lightsome feet,
Tumble and toss the hay in the heat,
Stray in the grass, stray in the wheat—
This the bliss of their burden sweet,
These the words they say.

———◆———

A MAN'S DEVOTION.

Thou dear, false-hearted, beautiful, frail child,
Though when thine eyes go wandering o'er my
face,
Searching for true love-tokens, I can trace
Sweet fraud in all their glances free and mild,
And in thy lips' light smile I find not truth,
Nor stedfast love in pressure of thy hand,
Nor in thy love-words music meet to soothe
A man's strong soul, clear as they run and
bland ;

Though I have read thy soul, child, through and
through,
And firm I am of will that no eye's glance
Could lull me into any amorous trance ;
Yet doth my love spring evermore anew ;

I dare not cast thee from me—thou, so frail
Who so hast trusted me, whom I so long
Have wrought and toiled for—lest thy foot should
    fail,
And thou be trodden by the brute-heart throng.

God loves the worst of us, His book declares :
Perchance 'tis godlike thus for men to cleave
To weak things He hath fashioned,—not to leave
The gem to perish for the crust it bears.
Howe'er it be, come, dear one, to my arms :
My summer glory in high Heaven is gained,
If only through the rough seas and the storms
Thou art borne back to God unscathed, unstained.

———◆———

CHEMIN DÉTOURNÉ.
BRITTANY.

SWEET was the little flowery lane,
    And planned to tempt away
A wandering foot, by fields of grass,
    And rippling fields of blé :
The honeysuckles through the hedge
    Made rich the air of e'en,
The brier-rose snowed its blooms on banks
    Of ferns and mosses green.

It led me round the haymakers,
  And through the shining wheat,
And all at once with woven leaves
  Screened out the light and heat,
And winding on by gnarled roots
  Of oaks, o'ercrossed a rill,
And swerved away, and curving clomb
  A tiny, bowery hill,
And down a hollow dusk and cool
  Of orchard gardens fell,
And lured me past a wayside cross,
  And past a wayside well,
And right before a cottage door
  Beneath a chestnut tree,
Into the light of two blue eyes
  God's love had framed for me.

————◆————

MISUNDERSTANDINGS.

AND you had wrongly read me, friend,
  And I had read you wrongly,
And so the hearts grew cold, and dead
  The souls that loved so strongly.

How blest we lived in olden days !
How glad the moments flew !
One gush of merry laughter, friend,
And life begins anew !

———◆———

OLD lad, old lad, thou art with me to-day
As sure as the lark doth sing :
Thine eyes are here, thy voice is near,
Thine arm to mine doth cling.

Let's wander out to the dear bright hills
And gambol awhile and play ;
And watch the brooks in ferny nooks,
And climb the clifflets grey ;

And I'll tell thee, lad, a tale of love
Will make thy glad eye shine,
And thou'lt shape for me the youngest dream
Of that wondrous brain of thine ;

We'll talk, too, of many memories,
Of boyhood bright of blee,
And the half-forgotten fervid hopes
That never fulfilled may be.

Old lad, old lad . . nay, lift thy face,
  That I may learn indeed
If thou hast *ever* left our Earth,
  Or *I* of Earth am freed.

———◆———

THE SINGER.

AH, my life has grown a song, a song,
  And the throat may not be still,
It is music, music faint and strong,
  And God must have His will.
Alack !—the rest of His singers gay
  He hath given them wings for mirth,
To soar and sing, to whirl and play,
  Over earth and the ways of earth.
O to flit through leaves, to swing on the bough,
  To do as an eagle dare,
To feel the cool flood catch the brow
  Diving adown the air,
To leap from the nest in the crag's high crest,
  And drift through shower and shine,
To make of the billow a moonlight pillow,
  To dance and duck in the brine,

In Autumn days through fathomless ways
  Fly to a sunbright south !
O to cross the plains of the ice and the rains
  And the realms of death and of drouth ;
To beat the cloud with pinion proud
  High over the stormy lands !––
Is it meet to walk on bruised feet,
  To clamber with bleeding hands ?
Alack, why cannot my soul made free
  To the fields of its God upclimb ?

Rest thee, rest thee : shall it not be
  In a little, a little time ?

––––––◆––––––

A LOVE'S THEOLOGY.

Is'ᴛ well that I with such heart's-jubilee
  Should love thee, hold thy face before my sight
Waking and sleeping, mould myself for thee,
  Thee only, searching for the truth and light
Just to draw from them thoughts and impulses
  That may upraise my soul into a life
More noble, lifting me by quick degrees
  Till I grow great enough to claim thee wife ?

Well so to cloud my heavens with this care
  That GOD is all unsought full many a time,
And quite forgot, and earth alone is fair,
  Nor dawns within me any dream sublime
Of worlds far off, or purer life to come,
  But here I live a joyous life, and drink
Deep draughts of love, and with free footsteps
    roam,
  Yet shirk no toil and from no danger shrink ?

Well to forget GOD's love for thine alone ?
  I know what thou wouldst answer from thy soul
Half-shuddering ; but I more bold have grown,
  For I have seen the narrowing mist uproll,
And seen the smile of GOD, and learned this truth—
  Man working out his destiny on earth,   ˡ
Fulfils man's love to GOD in very sooth,
  Matched with which praise and prayer are little
    worth.

And what is man's high destiny ?—nay, say,
  What, dearest, on this earth is thine and mine ?
Not to sit sighing for new heavens, not pray
  With lips and hands, but let this love divine
And heaven-born grow within us hour by hour,
  As GOD hath made our souls to love, and given
High tasks to work out *here*—a glorious dower,
  The very foretaste of the wished-for heaven !

He would not have us stand with upward eyes,
  Gazing, with saddened souls, through night and
    day
Searching for the Invisible in His skies,
  Disdainful of the mirth and innocent play
Which He permits His children in His fields,
  Among the joyous flowers which He hath set—
Nay, their shrill laughter to the Father yields
  A very bliss, be sure, and not regret.

THE RIDER.

I HAVE been a bold rider my whole life through,
  By river, by mountain, by mead,—
Foot fast in the stirrup, fist firm to the bit,
  And ever a gallant good steed ;

Never last in the race, ever first in the chase,
  Undaunted by dike or by drain ;
Taken leaps in the night o'er flood, o'er fell ;
  Ridden through tempest and rain ;

Swum through torrents, trampled in foam,
  On the crust of a crater stept ;
Traversed the desert in darkness drear ;
  Fleetly galloping slept ;

Sped at the head of a troop to fight
  Through the guns of the foe updrawn,
Riding out from the smoke in the end unscratched,
  With falchion red as the dawn ;

And so sure is it now that a hand of love
  Ever about me is wound,
I will plunge in the sea and dash into flame
  Lief as through open ground ;

I will bound through the lair of the tiger free ;
  I will trample the battle-dust ;
To the volleying rifles bare my breast,
  And laugh at the sabre's thrust ;

And when at the last to the utmost strait,
  The venturous life is driven,
I'll slacken the bridle, bend to the steed,
  Clear death, and leap into heaven !

A WAVERING.

Love, let loose ;
Set me free :
Ah, I choose
Only thee,
Only thee ;

Yet I wis
It were meet
Maiden feet,
Light with bliss,
Far should fleet,
Maiden eyes
Watch and wander,
Under skies
Alien ponder.
I would, lonely,
Yet one year
Roam,—one only;
Loose me, dear.

No, no, no—
Take thy will;
Clasp me so ;
Hold me still,
Hold me still ;
Be my king ;
Make me blest ;
On thy breast
I will cling,
I will rest ;
Though 'twere sweet
Many faces
Fair to greet,

Mystic places
Tread, ah, dreary
Mirth would be,
Beauty weary,
Save through thee.

———◆———

A LATTER-DAY PSALM.

YEA, we know Thou, Lord, hast created
    Earth and the stars and the sun,—
A work, though a thought over-rated,
    A god might rejoice to have done :
Ay, ay, but see in the doing
    Are manifold flaws and mistakes,
For sorrow is ever renewing,
    And the whirlwind shatters and breaks
The branches with endless breaking,
    Which things we should not allow
Had we, Lord, the world's re-making,
    We who are wiser than Thou.

L

Thou hast fashioned the bird and the flower
  And body of man and of beast :
They are weak, and the lightning, the shower
  Of the dawn, or the sword of the east
May touch like a light-flying finger,
  And lo, they are shrivelled and die :
Why may they not flourish and linger?
  Lord, we cannot descry.
What joy is in giving and taking?
  We would claim not the life we endow
Had we, Lord, the world's re-making,
  We who are wiser than Thou.

Thou hast filled up a chalice with poison,
  And forbiddest the lips to drink,
And if men in disdain of Thee moisten
  The mouth with the sweets of the brink,
Lo, death leapeth down like an arrow !
  Is it righteous the doing of this,
Or to make full of darkness, and narrow
  And thorny the path to Thy bliss ?
O, we would give poison for slaking
  Sweet, mild as the milk of the cow,
Had we, Lord, the world's re-making,
  We who are wiser than Thou.

The sins of the flesh are forbidden :
  Thou givest us eyes to see

The sin and the doom that is hidden :
  But why, if we will not to flee,
Claiming the help Thou bestowest,
  Why wilt Thou slay us for sin ?
Thou hast made for the highest and lowest
  Thy blessings too hard to win !
We would give men sleeping or waking
  Passions and pleasures enow,
Had we, Lord, the world's re-making,
  We who are wiser than Thou.

If Thou lovest man as Thou sayest,
  Why sins he, or why wilt Thou slay ?
If Thy sword is unsheathed and Thou slayest,
  Why sorrowest Thou for Thy prey ?
If Thou givest him thirst for a dower,
  Why lifteth he death to the lip ?
If Thou girdest his feet with power,
  Why doth he falter and slip ?
Thou art weak, and Thy tyranny shaking
  Tottereth : why shall we bow,
We, at a throne that is quaking,
  We who are wiser than Thou ?

Maim art Thou surely, and blinded,
  Yea, Thou art blinder than we—

Yea, we are infinite-minded,
    Yea, we are whole and can see ;
Thou art weak and Thy ways are a blunder,
    Folly the rôle of Thy deeds—
Come down from Thy chariot of thunder,
    And fling us the rein of Thy steeds !

For we, we would teach Thee a fashion
    None should be found to distrust.
In our hearts are love and compassion,
    We are pitiful, Lord, we are just ;
We would grieve for all sorrow and sighing,
    And lament with the souls that lament ;
And the living should laugh, and the dying
    Go down to their darkness content ;
And tears should be wiped from all faces,
    And pain should be painless, and sin
Sinless, O Lord, and sad spaces
    Ring through the night with the din
Of music and laughter and revel ;
    We would thirst not for tears or for blood ;
We would right the opprest, and the Devil
    Should come back and stand as he stood
Ere pride flung him down to abysses
    Of flame for his ruin—what crime
Is in pride, O Thou weak one ?   What bliss is
    In wrath ?   He was true and sublime—

We would go to his lair and restore him,
  Our brother down-trod and opprest :
We would drive all his torments before him,
  (Poor Devil !) and fall on his breast,
Bring forth the best robe for his raiment,
  And the fatted calf kill for his feast ;
We would give, and demand not repayment
  In love or in blood of slain beast ;
We would stoop not to punish with scourges
  The sons and the daughters of earth ;
We would stifle the wailing of dirges ;
  We would stay all the havoc of dearth ;
We would send down the rain in due season ;
  We would keep back the frost and the fly ;
We would loose not the storm without reason ;
  We would temper the sun in the sky ;
We would govern the thunders with system ;
  We would bind up the tides with a cord ;
For we are the people, and wisdom—
  Wisdom will die with us, Lord !

THE TWO THIEVES.

AND with the wondrous King are crucified
Two malefactors, one on either side :
And, now the King hath yielded up the ghost,
And these are left alone to gaze on him,
In tortured brain of either question comes,
And doubt, and fear, and wandering thought
    awry :
But chiefly in that evil one who railed
Dark dream and horror, this way menacing
The fair mute form long drooping in his sight :—

" Before the blackness fell, while yet he lived,
He to that other murmured with faint lips,
' This day thou shalt be with me in Paradise ;'
And lo the God of Israel hangs dead !—
Himself he could not save—and with him die
Hell, Heaven, and hope of Life, and sting of Death,
And still in cloud of darkness dwelleth man.

" For, if the man who set himself as God
Be dead indeed, then where in him was truth,
Where virtue, and where wisdom, or the power
To perfect promise ? Piteous were his days :

He would be king, and fell; he would be God,
And lo his dead limbs hanging in the storm !

" Shall I at word of his—the weak, vain soul—
Fear Hell ? What knew he of the Unfathomable
More even than I ? . . To noose a wayfarer,
Clinging for help to me, what subtler scheme
Than murmur of a lion in his road,
And, offering guidance, bind in reverence
His soul to me delivering ? Even thus
Spake he of fire for sinners, and himself
The way of life ; through fear and proffered help
The timorous souls so snared.

                 " Believed himself
The tale ? Then, wherefore, knowing sin's reward,
Sinned he the deadlier sin, making himself
One with the Mightiest ?

                " Or, if tempted sore,
Believing, yet through vain desires he sinned,
Then what ensample shall I find in him
Of selfless life, or sweet humility ?
What path through him for me from Hell to light ?

" Or one might ponder,—' Strong was his belief,
Pure, humble was his soul ; yet, brooding long

On God, and yearning towards Him, hour by hour
In commune, felt he closer to His breast,
Till, filled with that high presence, one wild
    thought
Beautiful, tenanting his lonely mind,
Went Reason out of doors, and, God that thought,
Self dwindling, God alone seemed self and God.'

" Then where was wisdom in that weakly brain ?
' I am Jehovah,' said he, ' Hell abides.'
When spake he truth, when as a madman raved ?
Sift me clear Reason's seed from Fancy's chaff.
Perish thy Hell, thy godhead, and thy dreams !

" And yet, when from my taunting face he turned
Meek to that other, promising rare bliss
Of after-life, fear slipt within my blood,
And harder were my tortures to endure,
A moment, as the vision of their joy
Flashed on mine eyes, and 'twixt us rolled black
    night
For ever, I cut off and isolate.
Never till then I grew unto myself
Loathly in sin.   For, as his patient eyes
Rested upon me, gentle in reproof,
A little moment seemed it that his form
Glowed like an angel's.   Hardly held I still

Reason uncheated : yea, I bowed my head,
As unto God's Anointed.   Then thought I,
' Surely that Heaven for weary lives were sweet ;'
And a great longing to make clear my soul,
Crouch in his love, and enter to his rest,
Turned sick my heart and whetted pain with pain.
But dead he hangs; and vanished is the hope ;
And yonder fool is cheated of his Heaven !

" And what if Heaven be lost to him or me ?
No joy, no grief hereafter; gentle sleep ;
The sinful man unpunished for his sin,
Or unrewarded for his strife with sin ;
The righteous left uncrowned for virtuous life,
Unvext with pangs for duty oft forgot ;
No hope of joy, but never fear of grief ;
No memory of love, but no regrets ;
No glad activity of brain or arm,
But never pressure of chain in irksome rest.
What larger bliss in life than perfect sleep ?
Surely we little lose in losing Heaven,
Hell following swift into the realm of nought.

" Yet might that hope of life renewed make strong
The faint, wrung heart to bear this weight of pain,
Now in the hour of death.   Ah, yonder man,
Still fondling the sweet promise, happier seems

Than I, and easier borne the pangs that wrench
His strained limbs from their sockets, as he turns
Appealing glances to that pale, dead face,
Or all but smiles, far-gazing through the blue,
As though he clutched that Heaven with his eyes.
Is he, then, strong though hope, and gains the
    dream
Colour of certainty, through working thus
A very miracle in heart of man?

" How many a time have I with patient will
Sat in the desert places, 'waiting prey,
Believing, ' Soon will come the laden mules,
With booty for my grasp, and prosperous men
Laden with gold and spices'; and all day,
Awaiting, blazed the sun or swept the wind,
And neither storm, nor heat, nor parching drought
Brought hurt, so sweet the contemplated prize,
Become a living presence, ruling sense:
And yet the day went down, and rose the moon,
And never ass, or camel, or wayfarer
Passed, or would pass.   So, so with yonder slave!
The falsest dream makes happiest the fool's heart.

"And, he being false, who seemed the holiest man,
And his a wildered brain they wisest deemed,
Shall I make treasure in my tortured mind

Of any thought of seer of old, or word
Of Moses or the Prophets, whom he came
Fulfilling—he, the latest lie of lies ?—
What knew they ?   I have laughed full many a
    time,
When men, my fierce confederates, peering stood
Into the thickest night unpierceable,
And some cried, ' lo, a horseman on the hills ! '
And some, ' a host of warriors moving near ! '
And some, ' a flock of sheep or drove of kine ! '
And some, ' a tiny shepherd boy afoot ! '
While not an eye could probe the dark, or range
Ten paces round.   Thus he, they, Abraham
Our father, Moses and the Prophets, so
David who sang Messias—one and all—
Peering into the impenetrable night,
Beholding nothing, dreaming many things,
And each one wisest in his own conceit !

    " Fools, fools, O fools !   Thus He that made
      the brain
Sowed it with madness ; He that formed the eye
Fashioned it subtly to behold no light.

    " He ?   Is He too a sprout of the brain's
      seed ?—
Jehovah—whom I cannot see, feel, hear ;

Whom prayer of mine ne'er moved ; who rules the
   world
For drunken frolic, it would seem, or lust
Of misery (hate's food), or fails to hold
His creatures firm from palsy of the wrist ?

   "Good call they Him ?   Whence evil in His
      world ?
Loving ?   Whence pain, whence hunger, sickness,
   death ?
Just ?   Where reward of virtue ?   Why the pangs,
Fierce punishment of natural appetite
He sets to snare His creatures to their fall ?
A Father ?   Where the help of voice or hand
To save, to guide, to warn, to wind from woe ?

   " Where found they Him in gazing through the
      night ?
What cloud the semblance of the Godhead bore ?—
A trick of Priests to fill their money-bags,
Of Kings to fright their people, and of Seers
To sway the mind of Kings.   Away with it !
I'll dread no shadow, tremble at no scare.

   " Then, wherefore fear the voice of Death, or
      shrink
Chilled by his iron finger ?   Wherefore groan

For days ill-spent, or turn repentant here
Of untold sin ?   What lost I through my sin ?
I hated, and 't was joy to let hate ramp :
I loved the scent of blood ; so murder drenched
With gladness.   Gained the virtuous richer prize ?
Nay : where has virtue ever won reward ?
I suffered hunger ; but the saintliest starve :
Sickness ; Jehovah's priests are not exempt :
Wounds ; yea, the godliest warrior no less :
And last this torment ; which the virtuous Christ
Has he not borne, and died as I shall die—
He, with the sensitive flesh, and vivid brain—
His agony more keen a thousandfold ?

" So, if it soothe my pain to mock them there,
Why pause ?   Why lock the mouth, or droop the
    lid ?

" But *that* desire has ebbed with ebbing life.
Let the twain be.   Too weak is life for scorn.
No laughter dawneth now.   With firm strong
    heart,
Death would I bear, but ah, remorseless pain,
Torture on torture, when shall come the end,
When the long sleep ?   For, ever in the mind
Throng visions, gathering, hideous, making weak
Courage and Will and Reason.   What is this ?

Have their vile dreams so dyed to their sick hues
All fancy, that the kindly face of Death
Grows awful from the darkness, and the heart
Yearns back on life again ? . . O joyous life ! . . .
They shall not slay me ! I will wrench my feet
Loose, and my palms clear of the piercing nails . .
Yea, struggling, writhing, twisted like the root
Of the snake-seeming vine-tree by the wall,
Break free, and fall, a mangled, streaming frame,
If only life a little while may hold
Here in the brain, till all be clear again !

"What if the Reason, warped and dulled with
        pain,
Deceived me ? Truth is ever hard to touch.
What if the reeling brain have clasped a lie,
And that was food I fought with in my pride ?
In dim uncertain night, it yet might be
Their keener eye caught truth, and I, who mocked,
Through weakness saw not clear in anywise.
When all is ignorance and wild dreams have sway,
Who stands with light for wildered Reason's help ?
Back, horror of fierce Hell ! Back, smile of Heaven !
God, hide Thy brows ! Off, grim and wormy
        death ! . . .
How can my soul believe if never yet
Thou gavest sign, or walkedst in my sight ? "

So the fierce unbeliever in his pangs.
But he that did rebuke him, in his heart
Communed in otherwise, upon the dead
Fair form and tranquil angel-face in love
Still gazing : and in pauses of his pain,
With hopeful spirit reasoned to the end :—

" I thought that when the storm had passed his
    face,
Like the clear moon, upon mine eyes once more
Would glow from out the darkness ; but he hangs
Dead, with droopt neck, and quenched eyes, and
    jaw
Loose on his breast, while we, the sinful men,
Are left to glare on one another's pain,
Hating each other in our agonies :
And when the spearmen come, in little while,
May my head too have fallen on my breast,
And darkness thicker than the storm's deep night
Made sleep my pangs !

         " And fiercer are my pangs
Than even in the midmost night of winds
And earthquake, when the plank whereon I hung
Swayed, rocking like the boughs of a living tree :
For now a great doubt fills me, seeing him
Dead, and his eyes glassed in the gaze of men,

And all that life lived vainly.   Lord, my Lord,
Wake; lift thine eyes; upraise thy lips, and speak.
Lo, all about the people rage and roar,
The town is loud with noise of wheels, and neigh
Of steeds, and clash of blades, and cries of men,
And the world sickens, and no help from thee!

    " What, if he lied to us ?   Ay, have they then
Visited him with death right gloriously,
Blasphemer, godless as that lewd vile man
Who taunts me with the leer of his scorched eyes
There—(devil, would the death were come at last,
Freezing thy body !   Mock me not : thyself
Art cursed with a like doom !)—nay, worse than he,
Throwing a deadlier insult in God's teeth,
And meriting worse torture, reaping less ?

    " Or, they that knew him, lay upon his breast,
Hoarded his words like honey, fought the world,
Have they that loved belied him in their love ?—
Then which of all the golden glorious dreams
That mine ears drunk, are mine for my soul's joy?
Which clasp, which spurn ? . . O black eclipse of
        day
In the waste wilderness, where never hand
Stretched or wild cry uplifted any help
May find in the wide air !

" It well might be,
Seeing they loved him, and to them he shone,
Love-glorified, a God. They lied ? What then ?
Then have they wrought fierce crime against High
    God,
And unto us His people. Worse, O worse—
Then is hope darkened, and God, wrapt in gloom,
Beyond His myriad worlds, unheeding lives,
Scorning the piteous brood of earth, nor speaks,
Nor doth reveal His veiled majesty
For hope or solace ; but we stagger blind
Across the deserts with no help, no change,
Plunged back to stubborn darkness and old night.

" It may be that the rumour as it rolled,
Part gathering, and part peeling piece by piece,
Comes with a changèd body. He was man,
Not God, save as of old through holy minds
God spake : and all his goodly promises,
His wise sweet counsel, and that love he breathed,
Were God's, and God held commune with this
    world,
He being with us.

"If these things were so,
Then likewise what is God's and what is man's,
What food for the soul's thriving, and what foul

M

With poison—for the mire and not the heart—
Who shall declare ? . . O agony of gloom !
Far, far from us the strong mysterious hands
That whirl the world in turmoil, and the arm
That guides through unseen ways !

                       " But if indeed
So spake he, and their record takes not hurt,
Then by his lips he said, ' I am your God.'

   " Can a God die ?   He droopeth mute and pale ;
No sound, no quiver of the mouth ; the wind
Waving the hair about the twist of thorns
They crowned him with ; scarce tint on either cheek ;
The beautiful strong body stiff and white,
Cooling mine eyes with its death-pallor chill.
If he were God, then dead in all men's sight
God hangs, a mockery, by his creature slain.
Could this thing be ?

                   " His life was pure and good ;
Wise was he, gentle, reverent.   Surely he
Uttered no blasphemy, nor spread false hands
Through lust of power, or pride, to clutch God's
      throne.
Nay, Lord, thy lips could breathe no lie, thy heart
For no ill lusted !

"What then ?   May it be
That other meaning in his words was hid,
Which the blind saw not, nor the deaf ear learns ?

" For, if the rumour of his words be true,
And not one least word other than he spake,
Yet might he, saying, ' Having known me, friends,
Ye have seen the Father,' speaking truth, yet speak
Quite other than they deem.   For how might God
To man reveal Himself?   O, not by form
Of His own presence, but by all things fair,
All beauty, and all virtue, and all truth :
And, having known him who was crown of these,
Him of the deep sweet wisdom and rare dream,
The heart of love and life of holiness,
So surely have we known the Father, seen
And felt Him ; yea, within that life of love,
That might of spirit, that just, fearless man,
Touched with our sorrows, fatherlike and true,
Have I not God brought near to me, to see
As in a little image, formed for eye
Finite to read, mind finite apprehend,
So lifting me to knowledge of that Love
Infinite, Power Eternal, in far heights
Of unknown glory dwelling, which though fixt
Beyond all comprehension of weak man,
Yet cherishes the lives of men It framed ?

M 2

" But, if their words unto mine ears with wings
Unbroken have flown, perfect at the heart,
And he with those dear lips nought else but truth
Breathed ever, and I may not read his thought
Thus, then is God far other than we deem,—
One, yet not one ; twain, yet not twain ; mere man,
Yet perfect God ; at war against Himself,
Yet harmony beyond all music sure ;
Slain by His own will for His wrath's assuage ;
Himself unto Himself up-offered,
Himself as man unto Himself as God,
Himself to help in self-inflicted pangs ;
By His own creatures for His creatures' guilt
Mocked and undone, that He through bitter death
Might snatch from Hell by His own will fore-
       doomed
Some souls whom He foredoomed no Hell to
       taste !

" How may my will in this keen agony
Find answer meet to soothe a heart perplexed ?

" Why hast Thou framed me for such fire of pain ?
Pain of the body, pain of the racked mind,
While pitiless across my brow Thy sun
Eats to the bone, and the poor, sick, live brain
In this red oven fights against its death ?

" If one would come and lay a cool fresh hand
A little while upon my frenzied head,
Or twine a green sweet bough within my hair
To quell the buzzing flies that light and suck
Their fill of fainting blood, methinks the mind
Might live less vexed with doubt and fretful dream,
And see, untroubled, with a calmer gaze.

" But, in my torment, I will test and probe,
Battling for truth. For if that tale of hope
He whispered were a promise false and mean,
And the rough taunt of them who bowed the knee
Just—' lo, this Jesus hath deceived the world ! '
Then better all these pangs of hovering death,
And terror of his imminent wings than that
Last swoop of ravening beak and piercing claw,
Wherefor I long as the parched runner yearns
For cool deep hollows of the brooks, to plunge.
Better to live unendingly, outstretched
Thus with my writhing limbs, and torn red palms,
Scorched by the sun-fire, beaten by the rains,
With charred and bitten lips, with eyeballs burnt,
Faint with long drought and hunger, wild of brain,
For ever dying, with life's blood-red sun
On the far verge lingering with lingering hope,
Than having heard him speak, and dreamed his
    dream,

To die, and see him not, nor hear his voice,
But prove him like the foulest false as hell.

" But who shall measure God, or paint His shape,
Or learn His substance, or His nature scan ?

" If God through all His universe breathes, feels,
Then he, I, all, dying, shall God too die ?
Who knoweth of the regions of His rest ?

" If God apart, invisible essence, lives,
And yet would speak to my corporeal ear,
Thrill me with kindred voice, make known His
    love
By channels of my sense through which love flows
From men aloof in sweet familiar streams,
Then how save through the body of living man
Should counsel, love, command intelligible,
Truth definite, come clear, to lift my soul,
Feed the frail mind, make righteous act and speech?
So might that body, having held His will,
Be cast to death (His will fulfilled at length)
As the fig-tree sheds its leaves, and yet God live.

" And what if He to teach the world of sin
Should thus expose Himself, who dieth not,
In bodily raiment, for their hands to touch,

Slay if they list, not loving love or Him,
Beauty, or virtue, or the star of truth ;
That so perchance hereafter, dreaming of it,
Man should repent and live, and pride's rough
　　heart
Break in remorse ? Who knoweth of His ways ?
Girt in with bars of iron, caged and cramped,
This way and that the fluttering, wailing soul,
Seeking the sun and far wide heavens for flight,
Dashes itself to madness, gaining nought.

" I, knowing not His ways in anywise,
Shall I aver, ' God cannot live as man,
Speak with man's lips, within such body move,
Even for His will's fulfilment ? ' How can I,
Who know not of His nature, judge His acts,
Declaring, ' this were foolish, such a deed
Mere contradiction to be laughed to scorn ? '
All that from which mine unaccustomed mind
Ignorant shrinks, beholding yonder form,
And pondering his life who named it his,
How shall my Reason in its night condemn ?

" Ah ! in this last dread hour, outspread in pain,
A miserable man, blind, ignorant,
Over and over in my worn weak brows
The mystery rolls, and all is darkness still.

" I know not all, and that which I have learned
Is rumour tossed from mouth to mouth, wherein
Truth lives perchance a fitful life, perchance
Holds perfect sway.   Will God who seeth all
Judge me for this, that struggling through the gloom,
I yearn for Him, yet know not where to find ?
Nay, God is merciful, and well I know
His awful might, and how He rules the world,
Fitting His works together.   God is just,
And when that Jesus spake, and in his eyes
I gazed awhile, love springing forth to him,
He seemed to pass from sight, and o'er me fell
The breath of God, and round me were His arms.
And in mine agony of death, though truth
Glimmer but faint and cold, I yet can turn
And, dreaming of His power, on that still face
Pore lovingly,—as there beneath the blue
Deep air, from which the clouds are driven down,
It hangs ; and, gazing, hold his promise dear
Deep in my breast; and, while the faint blood ebbs
Back its accustomed ways, and life's fair beam
Fades far and far, I still am strong within,
I feel God nigh, and death is sweet to drink."

So these, with no more light, in agony
Of body and of reason, musing, wait,
Till swoons the brain and death o'ershadow them,
Bringing what knowledge death in darkness yields.

THE VISION OF THE ISLES OF IMMOR-
TALITY AND DEATH.

YONDER it heaves at even and sunrise,
  The silent snowy Isle amid the blue
  Lone waters, ever in the day's warm hue
Dwindling, and when it withers from our eyes
The white clouds mark the region where it lies.

But now, as o'er the myrtled promontory
  I wandered, lo, in splendour of the noon,
  Above the waves its hundred peaks, outhewn
From mellow skies, rose clear and silently—
The silver-shining crownet of the sea !

O silent Isle of Death, deep slumber's mine,
  White wilderness of peace, low in the fern
  And odorous herbs gazing, I grow to yearn
For thy cold quiet dells, and inly pine—
There is no form, no loveliness like thine.

Like thine ; and *here* is beauty without end,
  Here quenchless Life, here laughter-loving
    throngs,
  Here music of sweet of strings, and subtlest songs
Of woven harmony, here friend with friend
Abides and parts not, never pain doth rend

The tortured body, never sickness mar
  Blue eye or rosy cheek, or tempest stain
  Light flower with moistened dust, or sudden rain
Chill roosted bird a-nights, or cloudlet bar
The path of moonbeam or of flickering star.

A wide-illumined land with never a cloud,
  Save when the mountain, golden-garlanded,
  Flings out a streamer for the sunset's red,
Or many-tinted droves to westward crowd,
To make the eye a gorgeous pageant proud :

For all day long the flashing fiery king
  Leans eager from his throne with eye awake,
  And the strong seas beneath him, laughing, shake
Their myriad-mirroring waves, that shout and sing,
Or start to life from sudden slumbering.

Far curve the mountains, like a bended bow
  Drawn to an arrow's tip with lusty arm
  (Another, touching end to end, might form
A perfect circle); and they stand in row,
A thousand bristling spears in purple glow,

A thousand craggy clusters, rough and round,
  Like black cloud struggling up the heavens ; and
    lower,
  Betwixt the mountains and the silver shore,

Fair vales with streams of clear delicious sound,
Pine-waving vales, green hollows olive-crowned,

Piled tracery of clustering lemon leaves
   Starred golden with fair fruit, and bowery roof
   Of perfume-wafting orange boughs in woof,
Pink peach and almond trees in flowery sheaves,
Which to and fro the wind in languor heaves;

Balm-breathing gardens, cool with jets of spray
   From fountains flung in many a rainbow bright;
   Broad statued terraces in lustrous light;
Flowers of all hues and odours; fawns at play;
And wildering birds that trill the livelong day:

Then by the sea's marge rise in lordly pride
   Palm-leaf and cypress-shaft; and then the wave
   In lulling music rolls by sand and cave—
The blue untroubled Sea outstretching wide,
The Infinite Void Sea that hath no tide.

Beyond the mountains, where they break and cease,
   Begins the plain to spread, with forest deep.
   Far-wandering meadowlands that seem to sleep
In the hot day, broad pasture white with fleece
Of sheep, and red with deer that browse at peace;

And then the vineyards, then the corn, the maize,
  The orchard-lands, the rivers winding clear,
  The dreamy lawn, the lake, the slumbering mere,
Vast prairies where the countless buffalo graze,
The belts of grove, the winding silvery ways :

And then again, upon the further side,
  The gray bright shore, the palms, the cypresses,
  The lulling music of the waves at ease,
The blue, untroubled Sea, outstretching wide,
The Infinite Void Sea that hath no tide.

And never doubt perplexes ; never care
  Furrows the brow ; to seek is straight to find :
  No task for toiling hand or eager mind ;
No fear of lurking sickness in its lair ;
No danger in darkness ; for the foot no snare.

Here is no mystery for the mind to pierce,
  For all is open as the vault of day ;
  Here are no bended knees or lips that pray,
Or any temple that the hand uprears,
Or sound of sigh, or track of any tears.

Slow roll the languid ages, hour on hour,
  Night on sweet day, sweet day on dreamless night,
  Season fair season following, with no blight
Of frost or fly delaying ; year with dower
For new-year, moving up with ancient power—

Time limitless, a blank Eternity !
O giddy depth of ages, gazing down,
Sick grows my heart, all hope is overthrown !
Remorseless tyrant, who shall strive with thee,
Who wrestle with thy countless hours to be ?

How many an age of years since first I woke
On this soft shore has slowly drifted by !
And then was the beginning. Where doth lie
The end of all ? When cometh the keen stroke
Like that which loosed the soul from fleshly yoke ?

There is no end : there lies the white, blank page :
There is no end, there is no pause, no end :
Into the trackless void my eyes I bend,
I peer around, above—long age on age,
The quenchless spirit's awful heritage !

And then the thought becomes a tyrant dream
Weighing upon my senses : yea, I cry
For the swift years of lost Mortality,
The little life of eld, with flickering beam,
When still a bourne before the eyes did gleam ;

The sweet pathetic life close hedged about
With barriers dark hiding the far Unknown,
Of which we vision made, with many a groan,
When sudden a loved face was blotted out ;
The tender life of love, and hope, and doubt,

The venturous changeful life that felt its bound,
  Sure refuge for the weary vacant soul—
  Not this long road of days with never a goal,
Far-stretching, endless, circling round and round,
Through which the slow foot journeys with no sound.

And round me are the faces changeless, fair ;
  A thousand years have robbed them of no tint,
  A thousand years no wrinkle shall imprint,
A thousand cycles shall not youth impair,
Or draw one streak of gray through raven hair.

Though myriad ages roll, to these no face
  Will added be, none ever ta'en away ;
  Shall never from our midst companion stray ;
Shall never new eyes dawn with tender grace,
To draw new love from the heart's holiest place.

There is no end, there is no pause, no end :
  No change that hath not been and yet will be;
  No birth of man, or bird, or beast, or tree ;
No coming or going of lover or of friend;
Through the long Void one weary way we wend.

Silent . . O silent Isle, afar, afar
  Flashing upon my sight, O dearer seem
  Thy cold clear mountains in the livid gleam
Of winter, keenly white as ray of star,
Than all the joys that in this region are.

There comes no dream of years unquenchable,
  There hovers not wide time with awful wing,
  There treads not any foot of living thing,
There for the pulseless spirit all is well,
There comes no thought, there death for aye doth
  dwell.

O that across the waters moving free
  From the dread future, awful, infinite,
  The weary dream of days that haunts my sight,
To thy far shores I might set sail, to thee
Journey along the silent tideless sea,

That, touching on thy sands, the throbbing breast
  Stiller and stiller in its breath might grow,
  Back to the heart the blood in languor flow,
Deep sleep upon the eyes be softly prest,
And the life drift to thine Eternal Rest.

TO ONE DEAD.

How did they lay thee when thy lips were cold,
  And all thy pangs gone over? Who pressed fast
  Thine eyelids on thine eyes? Whose hand in
  care
Gathered thy wandering tresses fold on fold,
Bright auriole of thy brows? Ah, who uplifted
  Thy little palms outspread in thy despair,
  To draw them to thy bosom? Who thy last
  Sweet whisper heard, bent low with bated breath
To learn thy will ere the frail links were rifted,
And thou wert borne far to the shoreless deep
  Whereon no pilot-bark ere journeyeth?
  Ah, who the cold white raiment o'er thy white
  Cold limbs drew, weeping in the lonely night,
Pillowing thy head for thy long lonely sleep?

Surely 't were just that thou hadst heard my voice
  Saying one loved thee—*I* loved thee—and my lips
  Had reverently kissed thy forehead pure,
And soul with soul gat folded, to rejoice
In dear love's liberty, ere thou hadst drifted
  Down the dark gulfs unsatisfied and poor,

And thy lorn life was rolled in that eclipse !
Surely 't were just that in thy dying sight
Mine eyes had seemed not to thy face uplifted
Cold, pitiless, nor that thy soul had lain
    Suffering the bitter wound of true love's slight !
    For what hath she who wears not on her brow
    Man's worship among women ? What hadst thou,
Poor vanished heart, whose years are lived in vain ?

I heard a cry break on mine ears, ' Behold
    This piteous end ! ' And a strange love was here
Flooding the vacant heart : and left and right
Stretched my lone arms, as the sick head is rolled
Hopeless of rest when weary dreams are thronging :
    And all day long and all night long, my sight
    Knew never vision save that shadowed bier
    Borne graveward, with thy pale reproachful face,
Wherein was frozen cold all love and longing,
With blank eyes gazing at the cloudy seas—
    Poor relic of a dear forgotten grace,
    Woman without the sweet of woman's life,
    Dead for dear love, poor child who wouldst be wife
And bear sweet children on thy cold white knees !

N

Let be. I know but as I know, and press
  Truth's icy lip ? Could I not lay my face
  Among the grasses born of thy decay?
What hope is here, or help for heaviness ?
Where glowed thy life-love like a sweet day's
    breaking
    The smooth-worn socket seals the succulent
    clay :
  Thy body and thy soul in one mean place
  Moulder together, mute, insensible :
There is no warmth for love, nor will for waking :
Conscience, whose life thy sensual-frame did feed,
  Reft of its food, surviveth not a spell.
    Thou wert. Thou art not. Wailing Memory
    Recks thy wan image for an hour. The sea
Of the world's life flings thee from it like a weed.

In vain thy mother bore thee, and in vain
  Nourished thy little limbs ; in vain thy feet
    Grew firm and thy tongue framed itself for
    speech :
In vain thy tresses thickened their dark rain
Around thy shoulders ; and thy budded bosom
    Bespake thee woman, ripening in love's reach,
  With lips for kisses waxen perfect sweet :
  In vain didst thou array thee womanly

For favour in men's eyes.   Poor wasted blossom
Lost to thy purpose, lavish womanhood
  Spent lavishly !   Now never use for thee
  Through the unprofitable ages.   All
  Thy pains were little worth, on whom shall fall
Never or one thing ill or one thing good.

Let be.   Let earth, and sun, and eager air
  Consume thee.   Let the grasses take their gloss
  Fed from thy breast.   Let the old elms arise
Refreshed with thee.   The children thou shalt bear
Are now the roses pinker than thy blushes,
  And the sweet gentians bluer than thine eyes.
  Earth in our ruin suffereth slender loss :
  As the sea draws his waves into the deep,
So are we hers, and with her palms she crushes
The life she yields.   Sleep in thy narrow cell :
  And in a little hour I too shall sleep.
  The worlds shall roll unwearying, year on year;
  Thy dust shall know not mine, nor feel nor
    hear.
Farewell, farewell, for evermore farewell !

A LOST GOD.

I REMEMBER it, years ago—
Many a sorrowful year ago—
The little church beside the sea,
Where with claspt hand and bended knee
I knelt in faltering prayer, and saw
ONE downward through the sunbeams draw,
With shining hair and raiment white,
Who laid a hand upon my head,
And bent, and kissed my lips, and spread
A sunset-splendour o'er mine eyes ;
And the blue waters and blue skies
Without the doorway wide for air
Were his, and he made dwelling there ;
And dearer seemed they for his sake—
More sweet the seabird's wing, a flake
Snow-white down-drifting in the blue ;
And sweet the shining skiff that through
The islets flashed in wind and sun,
And fled below the headlands dun
With waves and shadows along the shore ;
Dearer my love in distant lands ;
And dear the cripple at the door ;
And dear the beggar's palsied hands,

I called him king, I called him friend,
Father, or brother, who did bend
And breathe mild breath about my hair,
With ear laid close to heed my prayer.

I knew him then, whom now no more
Find I by wood, or weald, or shore.
God lives—but O unfathomable,
What shape, or soul, or thought is Thine?
I cannot learn Thy tongue, or spell
The letters of Thy name that shine
In blinding light across Thy sky.
I call. Thou yieldest not reply.
Thy worlds are round me, and the beat
Of Thy great heart beneath my feet:
I am a weed in Thy wave's breast
That heaves and falls in long unrest;
I am a leaf in Thy wide air,
With dust and birds blown everywhere.
Hast Thou dethroned him, or hath he
Died as the old sweet days for me?
Or doth the heart its own gods make,
To worship, cherish, crown, and break,
And him the love of boyhood bare,
Thee old disease and sin's despair?

A PSALM OF HOPE.

WHAT mean they, standing aloof, the people who
    watch us and weep,
  Tearing the hair in sorrow, and wailing and
    beating the breast?
Is it aught if the stream roll wide, is it aught if the
    waters leap,
  Swollen by snows, by the storm lashed white
    without pity or rest?
Have we not crossed many worse in our march, O
    God, as we follow
  Leader or lord who has led for a time and has
    fallen asleep,
Seeking to see Thee and feel Thee anear, going
    forth by the hollow
  White glens cut aloft in the hills, by the sands
    of the shores of the deep?
Would they bid us halt in our path? would they
    turn and go back in the night,
  And abide with the beasts of the field and herd
    in the dens of the rocks?
Nay, for our hearts are strong to the end, and
    we fear no might
  Of waters, or loud storm blowing, or horror of
    thunder-shocks.

We will on through the night and the storm, we
will march to the bountiful land.
We scoff at the lightning's glare, we laugh at
the torrent's roar,
As we plunge in the hurrying tide, and beat with
a buffeting hand
Foam and eddying flood, and stem to the further
shore.

For, ever thou drawest us on in the track of
invisible feet,
Through the crisp white mountain snows,
through the pathless desert ways,
By the grisly wastes of wood, by the blossomy
gardens sweet,
By the dry sea-wolds of sand, by the curves of
the tideless bays,
High over the spears of crag a-drip with the
sunset's blood,
By the shores of the desolate lakes that slumber
in tracts of death,
'Mid the flakes of splintering rock where the great
snow-cataracts flood,
In the fume of the watery flats, in the sulphurous
craters' breath.
Through sorrowful spaces and sweet we march
with resolute heart,

Nearer and nearer to Thee as ever the years
    roll by;
And more and more as we move in the wandering
    paths, outstart
  Signs that quicken the pulse, that brighten the
    fainting eye :
For lo, in the tremulous flowers we have found a
    shadow of Thee,
  In the purpled banners of day that flutter about
    the west,
In the droves of the flaming clouds blown nor'ward
    over the sea,
  In the hues of shining plumes, in the gloss of
    the leopard's breast.
We have wrung from the clenched crags the tale
    of Thy deeds of old,
  We have heard the hurrying spheres in music
    whisper praise,
And the leaves of Thy love have prattled, the birds
    of Thy love have told,
  And the streams that flash, and the deer that
    leaps, and the lamb that plays.
And we grow with the vision's growth, with the
    dawn of Thy love and power,
  Clearer of eye, and keener of ear, and stronger
    of soul,

And pain is lightlier borne, and light the driving
  shower
  As we push through storm and sun, and strain
  to the utmost goal.
And sometimes, fair in sight, will flash in a tide
  of light
  A symbol of peace to be, a promise of power
  to attain ;
For sometimes while we pause on a mountain's
  lonely height,
  Out of the stretching sea, behold, without
  shadow or stain,
A thousand marble spires, a cluster of domes of
  gold,
  Will arise and fire our blood ; or a land of
  loveliest dyes,
Bowery plots and streams and mountains fold on
  fold,
  In the sheen of the moon or sun, breaks sudden
  under the skies ;
Or a rushing music sings from far through the
  waves and trees ;   .
  Or odour of mystic boundless gardens floats
  anear.
Yea, we are strong in trust, we are strong in the
  faith that sees,
  And the love that yearns and clings, and the hope
  that conquereth fear ;

And dear, though rough, is the march, and sweet
  is the sound of our feet
  Treading in tune together, and gay are the voices
  blent,
As we sing in the lonely ways, and a mirthful
' measure beat,
  Brethren marching foot to foot ever on with the
  one intent.
O 't is good to strive and strain, and pain but turns
  to mirth,
  And we hail the worst with smiling lips as we
  march along to Thee;
For doing the deeds of men, we taste of the blisses
  of earth,
  We attain to the ampler life, we grow as the
  angels free;
And ever Thou drawest us on, and ever we follow
  sure,
  And Thou waitest our coming, we know, afar in
  invisible lands,
In the crowd of the sprits of light, in the realms
  that ever endure,
  To enrol us, born of Thee, at the last in the
  deathless bands,
To clothe us anew with strength and the fervour
  that shall not die,
  For the glorious deeds of gods, for the doing of
  works untold,

So soon as the years have run their span, O God
Most High,
And the season of man is spent, and the cloud
into darkness rolled.

— ◆ —

A DAY'S ENDING.

WHEN from thy last dear look I turned mine eyes,
As fell the evening, lo ! the mountain grey,
And in his heart a lustrous crimson lay,
A light of glory, a beam of subtle dyes,

That wistful stayed with him in lover-wise,
While from the West the sun had swerved away,
And though from wandering waves the moon did
rise,
Still loitered in his hollows, a lorn day !

So mocks false peace my heart so soon to pine,
So tarries dying gladness in my breast,
Light from thy light and virtue born of thine

About my soul, a lingering splendour, rest,
Or yet the old bitter dreams around me twine
To gloom the life which thine uprising blest.

Mentone, April 17th, 1870.

A PSALM OF DEATH.

To-day are Thy winds loose, and o'er Thy sea
  Flash through the leaping waves, blue, grey,
    and white,
Gleams from the muffled sun; and far and free
  Furrows the skiff with black side heaving bright;
  And up and down the winds the birds are
    streaming,
    Blown flakes that fill the skies with snowy sheen,
    Where faints the belted blue in the wave's green,
And the eye's realm becomes the mind's dim world;
    And round the sea's marge stand thy moun-
      tains gleaming,
    As gleams the water, with the spilt sun's dye;
Cool-flooding, fresh, the surging air is hurled ·
    Over my breast: and many a memory—
    Smile of soft eyes, and gentle voice's moan—
  Blent with the billows' thunder, the wind's cry,
Sways my tossed soul with dreams from Time's
    black deep upthrown.

A moment gone, as o'er the sea I stood,
  Where the green billows curve their maney necks,
Careering up the shore in thronging flood,
  And watched the seabirds, and the golden flecks

Of sunlight on the hills and waters playing,
The palm of a lost hand within mine own
Slipt lightly, and on mine ear a whispered tone;
The cloud of years unfolded, and the past
        Became as now; and I afar was straying
On fragrant shores beneath the blue expanse;
A boy's wound arm about my neck was cast;
        His young lips sang a vision, and his glance
        Glowed with a dear dawn-promise glad and
            free.
Love in my soul, new-woke as from long trance,
Stood with spread hands, wide lips, and wild
    expectancy.

Warble, of sweet girls' laughter made the glades
Awake in music; bright spring faces peeped
Upon us from the blossomed apple shades;
        And she was there to whom my love outleaped,
        All heaven shed from her, her spirit glowing,
        In pink soft cheeks, and eyes that saw not
            earth.
And round us gambolled in delicious mirth
Companions young and dear. And we did frame
        Vision on vision, wider, fairer growing
Of all that we should be, attain, and hold—
Knowledge, and love, and power, and sweetest
    fame,

Rest, and fair deeds, and pleasure manifold,
  Friendship undying, and unmisted joy . . .
Where, where are they, O Father, the young,
  bold,
Beautiful friends ?—where he that loved me as a
  boy ?

Clouds, mountains, fields have drawn them hence,
  to fade
Out of all sight and hearing.   Yea, I stand
With youth age-darkened in a world decayed,
  To weep alone.   For, lo, on either hand
    Are blight and ruin : lo, my fields are shattered,
    The winds my loves have trampled, and the rains
  Weighed to the mire ; across the sullen plains
Moan the bare woodlands, and the skies are drear:
    Around, the tombs of the loved dead are scattered
    With   sweet   names   carven   on   their   marble
    pale ;
And to and fro the burial-paths appear
  Moving, forlorn sad faces, sear and stale,
    Quenched eyes, wherefrom the light I loved is
    fled,
    And withered lips that moan, and throats that
    wail
The wreck of glad lost lives there dying midst the
  dead.

Unto Thee, Might Unfathomed, unto Thee,
Lord, do I cry.   O answer from Thy gloom !
What hope, what end, what void Eternity
Hidest Thou, what the truth and what the doom?
    Thou wilt not speak; Thou wilt not heed
        my crying !
Lone by Thy seas I stand, and hear the screams
Of the torn billows, watch the dismal gleam
The sick sun flings across the bitter waste ;
    While up and down the sea-bird flocks are
        flying,
And heaves the hurrying skiff in creamy foam,
And sullen clouds by the weird winds are chased,
    Down plunging into night ; and backward come
        The thoughts that choke my breath ; the long
            regret ;
        The old dead dreams that find nor rest nor
            home ;
The memories, the tears with which mine eyes are
    wet !

TO ———.

Thy hair that fell, a golden cloud,
  About thy pale face, flushed for gladness ;
  Thy laughing sea-blue eyes (a sadness
  Shadowing their laughter), as we stood
  Betwixt the aloes at the gate,
And heard the seawind prattling loud
  Through lemon-grove and orange-wood ;
    The touch and thrill of thy little hand ;
  Thy warbled words, and bosom's freight
  Of sweet farewells, as, half elate, .
    Thy brows were set to thy far land ;

And the regrets to know thee gone,
  And spring gone with thee, and sweetest days
  And dreams all over, and our bays,
  Dear valleys, mountains, waves, and groves,
  Drained dry of old delights—a bright,
Dread, cruel desolation lone ;
  Come back to me with the wind that roves,
    With shadows on the grass, and kiss
  Of laughing leaves, and gleams of light,
  And bear to me in pain's despite,
    A sadness dear as any bliss.

And I stood dreaming through the morn
  Amid the seawinds and the sun,
  Nor recked that in that hour had run
  God's mandate through the worlds, that swift
  The thunders from their lair should leap,
And in thy spirit despair be born,
  And death adown the whirlwind drift,
    As slides the spider from his nest,
    To glare with hungry eyes, and creep,
    And crawl, and daze thy soul to sleep,
      And suck the sweet life from thy breast.

Thou wert as the violets that blow
  Sweet breath below the olive-trees
  In winter; as rare melodies
  By wandering voices sung on the wind
  High up in a lonely mountain dell;
So fair, the heart would leap, and the brow
  Brighten for thee ; so pure of mind,
    The whole world, seen beside thee, grew
    Translucent as impalpable
    Pure thought ; a being whose white shell
      The spirit, star-like, lightened through.

Ah God! so many of the throng
  Of dead are mine and part of me,

I scarce could grudge the joy of thee,
To them, poor souls, who thus would keep
A friend so true for loves and trust,
If thou shouldst wander these among ;
    But I have wept, and I shall weep
    Tear upon tear, to think that death
So sweet a face shall draw to dust,
And one more faithful heart be thrust
    Out of all hearing of my breath !

———◆———

GLENS OF WICKLOW.

Glens of Wicklow, o'er the sea
Comes to-night a voice to me,
Bidding faint-winged memory hie
Backward to the years that lie
In a past so'drear and clouded
The sick heart, in sorrow shrouded,
Seldom dares to peer at it,
But where sun-born phantoms flit ;
And I roam, a blissful child,
Through grey chasm and ravine wild,
Hear your plunging cataracts cry,
Watch the wild-hawks in the sky,

Climb the frocken-tufted steep,
Down the dizzy gorges peep ;
And in boyhood's vision see
The sweet false dreams of days to be.

Glens of Wicklow, forest-crowned,
In your deeps a Spirit I found
Strayed adown the sunbeams golden
'Twixt the bearded branches olden
To the torrent's pools of gold ;
And her eyes, beneath the fold
Of bright tresses aurioled,
Held within their azure wells
Wanton smiles and wildering spells ;
And she chanted down the breeze
Songs that swayed me as swept trees
Tossed i' the whirlwind ; till I panted
For the things whereof she chanted,
Victory's wreath, and Wisdom's dower,
Glory of great deeds, and Power,
Knowledge, Fame for endless days,
The world's worship, the world's praise.

Ah, I think that truer-hearted
Lived I then, or ere I parted,
Following her wild music's flight
By weird ways through thickest night,

To find bitter her most sweet;
And to-day my pulses beat
To a music old and dear
Dropping dreamily on mine ear—
Sound of rivulets o'er the rocks,
Bleating of the mountain flocks,
Buzz of bees in blooms a-sway,
Laughter of light winds at play,
Blackbird's pipe and robin's trill,
Patter of nuthatch's bill,
Crash of boughs where the squirrel leaps,
Splash of troutlet in still deeps,
Herdsman's cry, and maiden's song,
Sounds that unto you belong,
And whereon my spirit fed
In the purer summers sped,
Finding life and goodliest rest,
Nursed on kindly Nature's breast.

Glens of Wicklow, torrent-cloven,
Round your streams my life was woven:
Even now, as faces fled
Of the dearest droopt and dead,
Flashing on the changèd brain,
To revive a soul nigh slain
With the loss of their love's dower,
And that withereth hour by hour,

Are ye to my heart left dry
By a drear Philosophy.
What of beauty here remaineth
From your olden influence raineth;
What of noble in me liveth,
That your far-off impulse giveth;
What of childhood's heart here stays
Is your boon of the olden days,
Folded in your mild caress,
Cared with loving-tenderness.

---◆---

AN APOLOGY.

In this delicious land of hills
    Some dear and hallowed spots there be,
With which a thousand joyous things
    Are blended in my memory:

Sweet vales where side by side we roamed
    Unseen, in happy childhood days,
And solitary mountains bold,
    And cool sequestered woodland ways.

To wind them with new deeds, new dreams,
    Their very loveliness would mar,
And leave me with a darkened life
    Unlit by any sun or star.

Then chide me not, kind souls, I pray,
   Nor think my heart is turned to stone,
If when ye thither wend, I stay—
   And go another time alone.

April, 1865.

———◆— —·-

A FOREBODING.

WHAT if "the grand old mountains" that we loved
Since boyhood's dawn was bright upon the brow,
And all the sights of wood and sea that moved
Our souls with impulses divine, should now
Become as powerless as an unstrung lute—
O my lost Heart of Hearts!—and never cheer
My life with memories amid sorrows drear!—
Methinks my tongue would be for ever mute
Of heaven-born utterance, and I should grow
Ignoble as a lightning-blasted tree
That never more will yield or leaf or fruit,
Tossing its lifeless branches to and fro,
And wailing 'mid the coppice wearily
Till the first tempest snaps it from the root.

September, 1865.

LUCREZIA.

(ITALY.)

O LADY, never felt I yet
That love was awful, that the spell
Of amorous eyes, intently set
    To speak what tongue were weak to tell,
Could chill the soul with sickening fear,
    Make fail the trembling limbs, and twine
The will with heaviest sleep, till here
    Thine eyes of light had gazed in mine;

Thine eyes of light that melt for love,
    Turned hither under passionate brows
By thy dark tresses crowned, that move
    Eager, or brood in languid drowse—
Thou on the couch reclining mute,
    Thy flushed, soft cheek against thy hand,
Thine arm's superbness bare, thy foot
    Slipt softly from its silken band.

Draw close the scarf over thine arm,
    Draw, fold thy shoulder's lustrous white;
Turn, turn thine eyes; break up the charm
    That holds me dazèd in thy sight;

Hide heavy lash and sombre cheek;
Release me, ere in wearying war
Swoons the sick life; for faint and weak
And reeling mind and senses are.

Thou beauteous thing, thy hands were good
    For love-caress, for dagger-thrust,
For poison-brewing; warm thy blood
    With fire of love and maiden trust,
With fire of jealous hatred vile;
    Thy kiss could life impart or death;
There's gloom and glory in thy smile,
    Delight and danger in thy breath.

I fear thy hate that sleeps unseen,
    I fear thy love that wakes for bliss;
Thou wouldst be queen, imperious queen,
    Clasp soul and body thine, to kiss,
To flatter, fondle, soothe, or kill;
    All service of the heart, the hand,
The lip, the eye, beneath thy will
    Subdue, to woo or to command.

I fear thee like a deadly dream;
    I fear thy dreamy eyes that charm
All power of thought away; I seem
    To drown in odorous oceans warm,

A singing 's in mine ears of waves
And sweet shell-music, my soul dies
As dies the flesh, the billowy caves
Opening and closing o'er mine eyes.

Though I shall tear me hence, and feel
Heaven's breath upon my burning brow,
Drink the sweet sunbeams, taste the weal
Of loneliness, yet, even as now,
Thy form, thy memory, then will cling
To eye, to soul, to inmost sense ;
I shall not find in anything
A charm to quell thy love intense ;

I shall not save my soul from thee ;
Thy love that awes me will waylay
And scare me through the world, will be
A fevering dream where'er I stray,
Past olive-wood, past glacier hoar,
In crowded street, in wildering plain,
By aloe-plot, by palmy shore,
Through tropic fire, through blinding rain.

IN VAUCLUSE.

ALL day along the crags I watch the sun
Linger, and they are joyous in his light,
But never yon dark cleft his smile hath won,
Where the poor flowerets languish in their night,
And fades the trembling fern, and shrinks the grass:
For pity or love he will not move anear,
Nor let his golden garments trail, alas,
High journeying through far heaven in lordly cheer.
So fail I for thy love; thou wilt not stoop,
While the bare places quaff thy beams in bliss,
To light the lonely hollows, where I droop
And my life sickens for thy faintest kiss;
And though the lost soul break to-night and die,
Still wilt thou pass, still live unheedingly.

A SOUL'S MYSTERY.

DARK are thine eyes and deep and still,
Like spaces 'mid the cedar-leaves,
That peep whene'er the dawn-wind heaves
And dies upon the plumèd hill—

Each space a well of living hue,
That star on star and world on world
Holds hid, betwixt the boughs unfurled,
In that intense unfathomed blue.

What veil they, sweet, my queen, mine own,
Thine eyes, my heaven ? what wildering spell,
What wisdom high, adorable,
What dreams, what light, what love unknown ?

———◆———

A SUMMER'S SORROW.

AND now the violet-blooms are dead
    We culled the winter through ;
Gone the anemones purple and red,
    And gone the bells of blue ;
Few hyacinths now in cool green hollow;
White jonquils fade, and soon will follow
    Hepaticas, waxen pale of hue,
The primrose in its bed.

Rarer than violets now thy looks ;
    Thy voice is hushed as night ;
Faint primroses in upland nooks
    May linger from the light,

The hyacinth yet in the wind may quiver
By ferny well or shrunken river,
   But gone the hands of tender white,
That bound them by the brooks.

Now blows the crimson gladiole,
   A fire in shady ways,
Thick rose-leaves in the light unroll,
   The vines are green with sprays,
Fresh ferns along the rocks are shaken,
The warm sweet eyes of summer awaken,
   The broom outshoots his golden rays,
The may is on the knoll;

New faces throng, new griefs are near,
   New dreams begin to dawn—
Come back and find the violets here,
   The blue-bells in the lawn ;
Come back and break the heart of sorrow,
With wind and light of lone to-morrow;
   Come back and show the cloud updrawn,
Old Anguish on his bier.

A NIGHT'S BEGINNING.

Aн, faded now the glory pure and mild;
Gone light and beauty; I no more am he
For whom the world stood opening tenderly
Wide arms of love, and Heaven approving smiled.
When thou wert nigh, all noble seemed my ways,
Stately the mind moved, came and went at rest
High thought; and, e'en when thou wert gone, for
    days
With sweetest light and music was I blest.
But now I know myself a mean man poor,
A vacant soul, a creeping wounded thing.
That beauty in thy beauty did endure,
That peace and virtue thou alone didst bring :
I did but triumph in thy gifts out-thrown,
And flaunt a borrowed splendour, not mine own.

SONG.

Where the pink hepaticas blow,
In a tiny mossy dell I know,
Hung in a mountain's piney crest,
Where the east wind and the west
Softly o'er the passes creep,

And sighing boughs the violets screen,
And, peering down the piney steep,
You see the palm-trees wave asleep
Beside the ripples that laugh and leap
In the curves of the Mediterranean blue;
Under the odorous pinewood green,
Where the hepaticas drink the dew,
O love, love, to be with you,
To-day, with you, and alone with you!

An April morn, a peerless one,
I, robed with the skies and girt with the sun,
Wild with the wine of the woods and seas,
Though the gum-perfumèd trees
Came down the jagged mountain-height;
And, hung between the sea-bays, found
A dell with pink sweet bloomlets dight,
And gathering, sang in love's delight,—
" Fly to me, bird of the winglet white,
Up from your home by sea-waves blue,
Over the mountain pinewood-crowned,
Fly to me here in the flowers and dew,
Sighing, and singing, and dreaming of you,
Dreaming of you, and alone of you! "

ON THE RIVIERA DI PONENTE.

FAREWELL !—I loved thee, joyous deep,
  In every pulse of wave and wind,
Thy laughing life, thy silvery sleep,
  Thy reefs of purple weed-entwined,
Thy green clear coves, thy bays of blue,
  Thy curvèd billows' necks of spray,
Pink in the sunset's lingering hue,
  Or rolling white in fiery day.

Ye knots of palms that plume the shore,
  Your branches wave with wildering grace,
As out of heaven's blue hollows pour
  The streaming winds through cloudless space ;
I joy to hear your whispers rise
  In languid leaf, in fringèd flowers,
Clear hung amid the violet skies,
  And clad with light through all the hours.

I loved to breathe the perfumed air,
  Beneath your boughs, ye light-green pines,
Most sweet when round the headlands bare
  The dreamy silent eve declines ;

I loved to lie from glare of noon
　　Among your stems' confusion grand,
And wait the dawning of the moon
　　O'er wave and rocky mountain-land:

O bowery olive-mantled vales,
　　Where summer lives through all the year,
Blown white by warm scirocco gales,
　　Green though the north be brown and drear,
Dear are your shades where violets spring,
　　Eyes dark with dreams and brimmed with love,
Where soon the nightingales will sing,
　　And soon will wing the callow dove.

O myrtled headlands stretching far,
　　Pine-crowned and girdled with the sea,
Sweet where the cistus blossoms are,
　　I called you mine, so dear to me,
Ye gardens of God's watering
　　And planting, where His footprints glow!
Ye to my soul high dreams did bring,
　　Long brooding where the rosemaries blow.

O, on your ragged rims, ye spears
　　Of rock, far up in seas of sky,
I drank the wonder of the spheres,
　　I quaffed the world's wild mystery!

Land of the noon ! my land of love,
Farewell !—I turn, soul-filled, to-day,
And satiate with sweets, and move
On honey-heavy wings away.

———◆———

LAKE LEMAN.

A REMEMBRANCE.

O the hot noons by sea-blue Leman Lake,
The moonèd nights ! O grassy garden-slopes !
O odorous, breathing luxury of flowers !
O beechen boughs that in the ripple slake
Your summer thirst, or wave at midnight hours
Across the peeping stars ! O cypress-copes
That swoon in the deep blue ! O cloistral, high
Shadowy roofs of creamy-tasselled limes,
Swinging the clustered bees ! O shrill sweet
chimes
Of unseen cicades dry !
O summer languor of bird-warblings low
That through the thick leaves flow !

P

Adown the hill-side came I through the vines
  That in the dust their purple clusters threw,
    Adown the vineyard paths and verdurous
    height,
From journeys by white peaks and clambering pines,
  And aged cities dim and plains of light,
  To find serenest bliss by waters blue,
  Lulled by the leafy music, peace to feel
This world of God in sounds and odours rare,
And manifold sweet colours, breaths of air
  That o'er the snow-tracts steal,
And glory of large light and boundless sky—
Deep peace to feel Heaven nigh.

And in those gardens, by green woven leaves
  Pavilioned underneath the domèd air,
    What gifts of earth were mine to touch and see
Of all the soul quaffs and the sense receives !
  For the great mountains, lifting silently
  Beyond the lake their vines and grasses fair,
  Clustered their craggy peaks and crowns of snow
Eastward, engirdling the blue water-deeps ;
And on the water, under piney steeps,
  Sailed winged skiffs aglow ;
And round the marge were belts of shimmering
  trees,
Mown lawns and winding leas.

And round the shores would throng from many a land
  Glad travellers, to drink God's wine o'errun,
    Wherewith Earth's brimming beaker foams
      for us,
Men fashioned by the moulding of His hand,
  Fanned by His winds and in ways marvellous
  Diversely tempered by His various sun,
  Fair, giant-shouldered men, or dusk of face ;
And women of black hair and hair of gold,
Talking in uncouth tongues or soft words rolled
    From lips of oread grace ;
And little children, of brown eyes or grey—
Bright throngs of wanderers gay.

There was soft noise of laughter from white throats,
  And carolling of kindly voices clear,
    And gambols of fair babes and glossy hounds,
And skimming of swallows and white pleasure-
      boats,
      And music swept from strings of subtlest sounds,
  And boom of bees in lustrous bells a-near,
  And luscious blooms of every sunny zone—
Blue, scarlet, creamèd cups, and balls of light,
Orange, and lavender, pink, crimson, white—
    By man's care found, and sown
By sunny and green paths, adown the shores
Wandering from happy doors.

It was delight, sitting in leafy glooms,
  With the mild scented breeze o'er lips and cheek
    Flowing deliciously and ebbing slow,
To drink warm breath of roses and thick blooms
    From those bright gardens borne; or, in the
    glow
  Of the full sun athwart a tiny creek,
  Watch the blue ripples diamonded with fire
Flash in great stars; or let mine eyes in love
Along the mountain slopes and bare peaks rove
  Up to the topmost spire,
Where the white snows of endless winter clung,
And the white cloudlet hung.

Sometimes with broad and palpitating wings
  On the near blooms a butterfly would poise,
    Pied wings with many-coloured eyes and
    rays,
Edged fairily; or bees with golden rings,
    Buried in honey-bells, their clangour raise;
  Or golden tiny wasps without a voice
  Hover and flit above the scented beds;
Sometimes a timorous bird on balsam sweet
Balanced itself, clinging with folded feet;
  Or flowers would droop fair heads,
Or open to the sun a languid lid,
With fervid eye half-hid.

Sometimes a boat with peasants drew to land;
  Sometimes a white-sailed skiff in view would creep,
    Tack in light wind, and steal away afar;
Sometimes a brooding shadow's purple band
    Belted the mountain, or an icy star
  Would sudden flash upon a sparkling steep,
  A white mist curl away to heaven, and fade,
Caught by the loving winds far up in cool
Seas of blue air; then in leaves bountiful
    Bird's trill, or laugh of maid,
Sweet, with the wind's voice, drew my senses
    home
Through the near groves to roam.

And when the moon above the waters stood,
  And all the folded stars hung clear and high,
    The dry leaves prattled, and the ripple talked,
And pinetree-tops grew white in the moon's flood,
    Then underneath the beechen shades I walked,
  Hearing the sighs of far lands, eye to eye
  With the illimitable universe:
Then was a strange sweet sadness mine—not
  awe,
For all seemed kind and true which mine eyes
  saw;
  Then would sweet peace immerse
Soul and keen sense, as with the summer air
All senses drenched were.

Such ways of bliss were mine at night and day
 By Leman Lake. But in the midst of these
  Hourly there breathed beside me, held my
  hands,
Leant on my shoulder, lived with me alway
  A Spirit and a Form from unknown lands,
  Whose touch was as a dream, whose silences
  Were thoughts borne in upon mine inmost mind,
Whose great, long-fringèd eyes, wide opening
Or lightly closing with faint smiles, did bring
  What never search could find—
Hope and deep love which read the mysteries
  right,
Unvext of fear's black night;

A Form of loveliest mould, a Spirit free,
  Merry at turns and glad with laughters clear,
   Or pensive-sweet like light of evening mild,
Or rapturous as the dawn on summer sea ;
   Pure-hearted, playful as a rosy child,
   Yet wise with wisdom of the elder year;
   Who knew as the world knows, yet had eye
   and heart
To love and see as the world seeth not;
Sitting in shade, or over grassy plot
  Treading, from men apart,
Beside me ever did It seem to dwell
And o'er me breathe Its spell.

It was not human wholly or divine,
    But of the very heaven and of the earth,
        And breathed of all things sweet that round me
        were,
Being of them, as of clustered grapes the wine.
    And, dreaming back upon those summers fair,
        It seems the truest source of all my mirth,
        Real as the flower I press beside my lip,
True as the wind's voice or the water's word—
A thing of life, like the air-winnowing bird,
    Gold-girdled bees that sip
Hid honey, or the fiery sun above,
Father of life and love.

It was the Spirit of the mightiest dead,
    Who there have felt the glory and mystery,
        The love, the power, the light, or striven to feel;
They who around thy shores, O Leman, fed
        The deep heart's hunger, wild, unquenchable,
    Among the shadows of the things that be
    Out of all sight and hearing : Spirit pure
Of lives in failure most magnificent,
Great in the baffled will's sublime intent,
    Whose thoughts, whose dreams endure,
Speaking   from   forth   the   mountains   and   the
    caves,
As with a power that saves.

I knew thee, Spirit, and have known thee. Yes,
  When the dear lives fade like a leaf and fall,
    Thy hand is laid upon my lips, thy smile
Rebukes me mournful ; ah, thy true arms press
    Round the droopt neck when trusted brethren
      vile
    Show the beast's heart, and fill life's cup with gall;
    Ay, when the eyes beloved with sudden gleam
Reveal how mean the love for which I pine,
Then thine eyes brimmed with true love look in
      mine,
    Thy face, a fairer dream,
Before me lives, and I may laugh to death
False eyes and serpent-breath.

Man in man's likeness loveth all things dear:
  Thou art the visible raiment of all thought,
    All peace, all hope, all beauty I have drained
From the brimmed founts of being ; messenger
    Thou from the world, springing to love out-
      rained
    On all of sweet Heaven to my door has brought;
    Bright essence of all beauty and all good ;
Subtle response of love to the soul's kiss ;
Fair intercessor between that which is
    And that which is not mine ;
Word palpable in form, gleaming intense
On the life's inward sense.

And I sigh, yearning for thee, Spirit sweet,
  Even as in sickly autumn of the west,
    To-day, beside cold seas at veiled noon,
I yearn for that blue lake, the light, the heat,
    The glory of clear eve and golden moon,
  My draughts of loveliness and my soul's rest.
  Where bidest thou, and wherefore art thou fled ?
And shall I find thee, seeking up and down ?
Lo, the skies darken, and the moors are brown ;
    And all sweet sounds are dead ;
God hath withdrawn Himself in dusk and cloud,
And troublous storms are loud.

THE END.

This is Life. –

If we die to day, the Sun will shine as brightly, and the birds sing as sweetly tomorrow.

In a few years not a living being can say. "I remember her." We lived in another age, & did business with those that slumber in the tomb.

This is Life.
How rapidly it passes!

UGONE: A TRAGEDY.

BY GEORGE F. ARMSTRONG, M.A.

A New Edition. LONGMANS & Co. *Price 6s.*

---

wrongs brooding in his heart, wrongs done to his house in past time by enemies who still live and flourish, wrongs daily suffered by himself from the society which spurns him in his fallen fortunes. As the scales are trembling in suspense, there come new and unpardonable injuries to turn the balance against the better cause, and the play, which is of a very sombre hue, ends in crime and disgrace. . . . There is dramatic power in *Ugone*. . . Though the drawing of the hero's character does not make a very favourable impression on our judgment, the minor personages—*Marina*, for instance, a thorough Italian woman—are well conceived. We like Mr. ARMSTRONG best in his descriptions of scenery. . . . But the whole is carefully written, in language well chosen, with metre that seldom fails in melody."

From the "WESTMINSTER REVIEW."

" *Ugone* will, we are afraid, not meet with so many readers as it deserves. . . Certainly a reading drama does not hit the taste of the day, even when written by the most popular authors. . . . *Ugone* deserves to be an exception. . . . Great powers of description."

From the "STANDARD."

" [He] has both power and passion, as well as originality ; and though the present age has more sympathy with burlesque than tragedy, readers will be attracted by the vigour and boldness of the story here told them. A modern tragedy, with the scene cast in Italy, is in itself alone a sufficient claim to notice. . . The work of an educated mind . . . real poetic taste and feeling."

From "PUBLIC OPINION."

" This is a five-act tragedy by a young writer already favourably recognized among the rising generation of poets. Among these, judging from the present as well as earlier performances, Mr. ARMSTRONG will, in all probability, take a marked place. He can conceive a subject as a whole, and not merely as a congeries of fragments, which is more than some poets, even of no inconsiderable repute, can achieve. His language, too, is terse and forcible ; his descriptions of scenery vivid and picturesque, and his personages . . . are instinct with life."

From the "ORCHESTRA."

" After pale, colourless imitations of Tennyson, and the mock materialisms which follow in the track of Swinburne, it is refreshing to come upon the evidence of original power in a poet. Mr. ARMSTRONG may claim that honourable designation without impeachment. He is not moulded, and is only slightly coloured, by the new schools. In his verse there are no purloined conceits, no runnings in grooves, no echoes from a richer muse. . . . His verse is melodious, and rich, and attractive. This is no slight praise, to say the workmanship is good, and yet recalls no recognized master. Very few writers of the day could take up Mr. ARMSTRONG's subject and make it tolerable . . . A tragedy in blank verse, and numbering two hundred and fifty pages! Respect for Mr. ARMSTRONG quickens into interest. The poet has a quick eye for character, and an artist's faculty for reproducing it. The personages of the drama assume an individuality, and preserve it. It is not that the author labels them or insists on their attributes, but that their own speech bewrayeth them. This is true dramatic art. . . If his work is over elaborate, the elaborations are good; if his arena is crowded with personages, these personages have each his own life and character. . . The murder is artistically represented off the stage, as it were. . . The subsequent scenes of contrition and horror are full of force. . . There are several sub-histories which march side by side with the principal story; but these are too com-plicated to relate. . . . We have quoted one speech for its vigour and imagery. Let another extract be a sample of delicate landscape-painting, such as occurs now and then to soften the pressure of action and the tumult of rival interests. . . . This is a perfect pic-ture of north Italian scenery, painted with the hand of a master. But *Ugone* was written in Italy, and the passion and music of its pages have a savour of the land."

From the "EDINBURGH COURANT."

"We have looked forward to this volume with more than ordi-nary interest. Mr. ARMSTRONG's first volume attracted a consider-able amount of attention, and was acknowledged by competent critics to show more real power and true poetic insight than any first effort had done for some time. The genius of which his lamented brother Edmund had given proof before his too early death, no doubt enlisted for the *Poems* warm sympathy; but we had only to dip into *Coragene's Temptation*, and some of the exquisitely beautiful minor pieces, to recognize that the poet's mantle had fallen upon both the brothers. . . The power, passion, force, and pathos of *Ugone* are so great, that we do not require to ask our readers' for-bearance while we take them rapidly through some of the principal scenes in it, and give them extracts from a drama which they ought to read, and, reading, will learn to love. . . . Richness of thought, force of utterance, power of description, are the charac-teristics of Mr. ARMSTRONG's genius. . . . His verse is copious, free, unrestrained, passionate, vigorous; now pathetic, now tender; always musical and beautiful. . . . We are afraid we have not been able to convey to our readers an adequate idea of the drama. The canvas is so crowded, the scenes change so quickly, the lights and shadows come and go so fast, that it is not easy to give a good account of it without seemingly destroying the artistic roundness of the picture as a whole. We hope to hear soon of Mr. ARMSTRONG again."

From the " BIRMINGHAM GAZETTE."

" We have received *Ugone: a Tragedy*, from the pen of GEORGE FRANCIS ARMSTRONG, brother of the late Mr. E. J. ARMSTRONG, whose poems attracted such favourable criticism some four or five years ago. Poetical talent appears abundant in this family. This present writer has published a volume of miscellaneous poems of great merit, and he now presents to the world a tragedy original in its conception, scholarly in its execution, and stately and elegant in its style. We leave to abler critics the analysis of this long story, which is, we learn, for the most part based on fact. Its scene is laid in Milan. . . Individuals of all nationalities figure among its *dramatis personæ*, and there is abundance of scope for the display of character, scope of which the author fully avails himself."

From the " DARK BLUE MAGAZINE."

" The gifted author of *Ugone* tells us in his 'apology' that the main portion of this drama is based on fact, and further, that the characters are sketches from life. This statement finds an echo in almost every scene of the poem, for it is no exaggeration to say that nowhere in this drama do we meet with that unnaturalness and utter improbability of incident which mars so much the development of plot in so many of our recent dramas; and that everywhere we find the *dramatis personæ* not merely speaking a language most consistent with their characters as presented by the poet, but acting in a manner consistent with the natural conditions of the circumstances in which they are placed. The terrible tale of this tragedy may be told in a very few words. . . From the merits of the poems before us, we are induced to place a high value on the poetical abilities of the author; almost every scene of it thrills us with terror or melts us with pity. Power is the special characteristic of Mr. ARMSTRONG's poetry. . ."

" . . . The powerful current of his poetry is not the majestic might of the calm, broad, deep river which flows on, reflecting in its placid bosom the overhanging beauty of the heavens, and the surrounding brightness of the earth; but it is the unrestrained and impetuous strength of the mountain torrent-stream, overflowing its banks, and sweeping away in its resistless deluge every object that it meets. . . It bears the undoubted impress of genius, as none will doubt who feel the pulse of poetry in their blood. The love scenes between *Adelaide* and *Ugone* are pervaded with the highest and purest inspirations of passion ; and the last scene, where *Adelaide* dies in the arms of her lover, reaches the height of intense tragedy, and reveals a degree of power on the part of the poet rarely equalled by the most popular poets of the day, even in their best passages."

From the "DUBLIN EVENING MAIL."

"It is with no small pleasure that we now hail Mr. ARM-STRONG's second appearance in print. The drama before us gives evidence of a mental advance, quite wonderful in so short a time. We heartily congratulate Mr. ARMSTRONG on his year's work. . . . The plot has the merit of originality, and is remarkably well worked out, the action steadily advancing, and the interest deepening from first to last. . . . The whole drama is a bold, and in a great measure, successful attempt to idealize some aspects of modern life. The dialogue is happily managed throughout, the author giving us good sonorous dramatic blank verse, and, what is perhaps even less common, good dramatic prose. . . . [We] come to Scene VI. of the Fourth Act. This we think the greatest scene in the drama; in it the whole horror of the tragedy culminates. . . . The whole scene is full of weird gloom and stormy passion. . . . We wish him [Mr. ARMSTRONG] a hearty godspeed in the career which he has chosen, and we shall watch this career with sympathy and interest."

From the "DAILY EXPRESS" (*Dublin*).

"Mr. ARMSTRONG has already gained for himself a name by his volume of poems, published last year. . . . The scene [of *Ugone*] is laid in Italy, and the southern warmth and richness of colouring that pervade the whole, give it a singular attractiveness. In pourtraying character, Mr. ARMSTRONG is peculiarly happy. A large number, perhaps too large a number, of *dramatis personæ* are introduced, and yet none are mere sketches. They are portraits which stand out boldly in strong relief, and are as far from anything of indefiniteness as they are from being caricatures. The hero, *Ugone Bardi*, is a thorough Italian, strong and fiery in his passion, whether of love or hate. . . . Perhaps the finest and most original conception of character in the work is that of *Francesco*, the artist brother of *Ugone*. . . . The female characters are well conceived and worked out. . . . The earnestness and purity of tone throughout the work are especially worthy of praise. Appealing, as it does, to the intellectual, and not to the animal, part of our nature, this tragedy of Mr. ARMSTRONG's is a strong protest against a class of writing that has gained but too large a show of popular favour."

From the "FREEMAN'S JOURNAL" (*Dublin*).

"The plot is skilful. . . He has very considerable command of language . . . his thought is not common-place . . . his images

are suggestive and unconstrained . . . his lines are accurately
measured, and his sentences are neatly balanced . . . there is not
a bit of bad sense in the whole 250 pages; and this itself is uncommon in a young poet. . . . Good taste . . . sound sense . . .
an energetic capacity."

From "SAUNDERS' NEWS-LETTER" (*Dublin*).

"The ability manifested in the earlier published poems of this
gentleman has progressed to a fulness in the tragedy of *Ugone*. . .
That *Ugone* has some blemishes . . . cannot be disputed ; but
these are few in comparison with its beauties of diction and truth
of characterization. Then it has the genuine ring of poetry, not
bejewelled with over-adornment of imagery, but replete with
sentiment charmingly expressed, and suitable to the situations and
feelings of the actors. . . . It is curious, and pleasantly curious, to
find dramatic and poetic instinct so indicative of genius throughout
this tragedy. It is felt as an odour in lines of exquisite fitness; it
rises to grandeur of utterance in the expression of noble and ap-
propriate sentiments, and leaves upon the mind of the reader
the grasp of a genuine poet. . . . We cannot but congratulate Mr.
ARMSTRONG on the production of a genuinely artistic work, and
we hope further to hear of him. . . . We must think [him] a
very young man, and, therefore, we have large hope in his future
productions."

POEMS BY GEORGE F. ARMSTRONG, M.A.

SAINTE BEUVE.
(*From a Letter of the 26th January*, 1869.)

"Un poëte d'une sensibilité vive et grave, presque austère, et
avec des accents de tendresse. . . . Ce poëme lyrique qui s'ap-
pelle *Un Dechirement d'Amitié* a remué en moi bien des fibres.
Que de pensées ! que de nuances ! que de vers saisissants par
le naturel, poétiques à la fois par l'image et par la vérité des
détails!—

'The shadow crossing o'er the gravel-walk
Will draw thee to thy window' . . .

Et de beaux vers simples qui s'élancent :—

'Thou wilt not gladden with the dawn of Spring!—'

. . des accents qui font tressaillir jusqu' à la vieillesse, et qui lui
arrachent des soupirs."

From the "REVUE DES DEUX MONDES."

"Son livre le fait connaitre pour un esprit sincère, profondement
religieux, mais n'accordant sa confiance à aucune des églises ou des
sectes de son pays, pour un cœur aimant qui s'epanchait dans des
vers plutôt tendres que passionnés."

7

From the "LEADER," *January* 30, 1869.

"His blank verse is made subtle and suggestive by the flow of a rich and copious rhetoric, though repressed with considerable artistic power, and moulded after a fashion which never suffers its implications or its direct meanings to grow vague or involved. . . . He spiritualizes his aspirations with pure and exalted thoughts. His direct appeals to the Almighty, his musings on Christ, are all noble. Even the occasional references to his slight and reasonable scepticism are rendered fascinating by their melodious utterance, and beautiful by their rich inlay of wise, poetic doubt. The second poem in the book, called *Sundered Friendship*, is full of exalted pathos. The tenderness that vibrates throughout the whole length of the verses appeals with an irresistible power at its close. Mr. ARMSTRONG has learnt the secret of making his pathos unerring, by colouring it with the eloquence of a highly-wrought belief in the mercy and love of the great Father of all. The hush of a deep religious feeling renders solemn the closing stanzas of this poem. . . . It falls very sweetly after the passionate outbursts that sometimes swell the lines into positive sublimity. . . . *Coragene's Temptation* is a truly forcible dramatic fragment—remarkable for its sustained vigour of treatment. . . . Its merit lies in the subtlety with which the various passions, inspired by a love that would not and yet would, are developed—the abruptness of their transition necessitating a careful discrimination to prevent the separating periods being too marked, and the emotions consequently rendered abnormal by glaring contrast. . . . Quotations from such a poem as this, whose merit is its artistic entirety, embracing the lights and shadows of frequent and varied impulses of passion, can convey but a poor notion of the cause of our admiration to the reader. . . . But to our minds the sweetest and most original poem in the collection is that entitled *In the Dance*. Anything more airy and delightful, anything more tragic in its abrupt finish than this composition, cannot be imagined. It is one poem, however, of many that are more or less piquant, dramatic, or subtle. . . . To all lovers of poetry we commend Mr. ARMSTRONG's volume as one of the choicest contributions to the poetical literature of the period the last half-dozen years have seen."

From the "ATHENÆUM."

"[He] has great command of language and a faculty for writing in verse with firmness and force of utterance. . . . *Coragene's Temptation* is the best thing in the book. . . . It is argued out as Mr. Browning argues for his characters. A Saint, living in a wilderness, is in love with a beautiful and innocent girl. His strugglings against earthly passion, his belief in the mortal sin he is committing, and the subtlety with which the temptation glides into his heart and brain; the mixture of love and the base fear of injuring his own soul; the gentle, worshipping love of the girl; are very forcibly and well described. . . A power of understanding and sympathizing with the contradictions and moods of thought in a human soul at war with itself."

From the " SPECTATOR."

" The writer has a style of his own. It displays, indeed, the fervent audacious rhetoric which distinguishes our youngest school of poets, but it has a sufficiently marked individuality. . . Repose is a quality which it would probably disdain. Will the writer, whom we judge to be a very young man, excuse us if we advise him to mingle a little more thought with his passion? We like *Through the Solitudes* as well as any of the poems. It begins with some vigorous lines . . . and the horror of solitude and death which comes upon the traveller when he reaches the lonely moor is described with no little power."

From the " LONDON REVIEW"

" A bold and nimble fancy; affluence of language; a ready supply of images. . . . The cast of his mind is essentially lyrical, and his poems consequently belong to the lyrical order. They have the characteristics of warmth and movement—lacking, almost as a necessity, repose. Perhaps the speciality of the book is a certain independence of view and tone, which gives much zest to some of the pieces."

From the " DAILY TELEGRAPH."

" Three or four years ago died Edmund J. Armstrong, whose poems have since been edited by his brother, Mr. GEORGE FRANCIS ARMSTRONG. The latter now publishes a volume of verse of his own, simply entitled ' *Poems,*' which is likely to attract attention. . . . We shall not be surprised if this little volume causes a considerable fuss. . . . It is certainly well deserving of examination."

From the " QUEEN, THE LADY'S NEWSPAPER AND COURT
CHRONICLE."

" His brother Edmund lived only long enough to reveal his poetic genius to the world. Happily there is still in the family a genuine singer, and one whose utterances cannot fail to please. The versatility of his talent appears in the varieties of composition and subject which he has chosen and handled so well. At one time an airy quaintness distinguishes his manner; at another his march is measured and solemn; sometimes it is the playfulness of the child, and sometimes the sternness of the warrior. Here he deals with worldly themes, and anon he treats of high matters of religion. Sometimes he rhymes in elegant lyrics, and sometimes writes dramatically and in blank verse. There is a certain boldness and originality in his conceptions, and an aptness in his similes which is remarkable. Take as an example—

'Ay, Time will draw thee from me, as the sea
Draws weed or shell flung up from glutted graves
To the starved sand, and runs in mockery
Back, laughing in the hollows of his waves.'

. . . The felicitous use of his epithets is one of his peculiar excellencies. . . We have found so much good in this volume that we will not even allude to incidental blemishes, which are indeed but few. It is encouraging to meet sometimes with poetry amid the forest of verse produced in our age. Let us repeat our assurance that there is poetry in this book, and we conclude by warmly recommending it."

From the "ABERDEEN JOURNAL."

" It is a pleasure to dip into a volume such as this now before us. The author—evidently a young man—has struck out of the old beaten paths, and in a measure at once original, melodious, and refined, gives us many poems which will bear to be read once and again—which is saying a good deal as poetry goes now-a-days. At one step the poet has taken his place among our true poets, and has gathered around him a rapt and listening audience. To give some idea of the volume, we make one or two extracts, advising our readers, however, to see the work for themselves. The opening poem entitled *Slain in the Forefront* [is] tender and touching, evidently referring to a brother of promise who died, ... and whose writings, published some two or three years ago, were so favourably received by the press. In *Iesus Hominum Salvator* are verses that carry the reader along with them, and wake in the soul better and holier feelings. . . *The Christ* has the true ring of poesy in it. . . *Coragene's Temptation,* a finely-written poem in blank verse [is] the masterpiece in the volume. *Babble* has all the merry playfulness about it of the mountain rivulet addressed. . . . We take leave of Mr. ARMSTRONG, trusting, nay confident, that advancing years will more than fulfil the promise given in this his first literary venture."

From the " FIFESHIRE JOURNAL."

" This volume is one of great promise, by a gentleman gifted in no small degree with a vivid imagination, deep susceptibility, insight, and a sweet and easy power of expression. The brother of the author died when quite a young man, and just when his undoubted power as a poet came to be recognized by the critics; and touching traces of suffering for, and yearning after, a dead brother, are visible in many pages of the present volume. The poems entitled *The Invisible, Iesus Hominum Salvator, A Latter-Day Psalm,* and the *Most Highest,* are full of spiritual depth of meaning, and could only have come from the pen of one who has pondered long on some of the greatest truths of our nature. Mr. ARMSTRONG's longest and strongest poem is entitled *Coragene's Temptation.* The poem is passionate and powerful throughout. Some of the minor pieces have a delicious lyrical ring in them. In the *Ditty* our author is particularly happy, especially in the verses beginning ' O love, thou'rt like the dawn-wind that sighs across the sea,' ' O love thou'rt like the flowing of wine on fainting lips.' *Kisses* is a little gem in its way. The *Echo-Song* has the gay sportiveness and playfulness, in its conception and form, which we feel when, by ' Glacier blue and snowy horn,' we seek in the echoing hills a response to our souls' joy and mirth. . . . These lines in *Babble,* too, strike us as having something of the music of the ' silvery rivulet' he is addressing. . . . There is a pretty conceit in *In the Studio ;* and in *In the Dance* there is the whirl and excitement belonging to its subject, the end of it being particularly well managed. *A Demonstration* tells a great truth in a neat and effective, though outspoken way. . . . We conclude in our author's words, wondering, as we always do when lifted for a little above the world of sense and passion, from which we are ever endeavouring to escape —

> ' I marvel what the Father keeps from us
> Beyond the great wide sea, where the winds rove
> Lonely, and never ship hath sail'd.'

This [book] may be taken as a guarantee of the possession of real poetic power, which, we trust, will soon blaze out in some further proof of it."

From the "EDINBURGH DAILY REVIEW."

" This volume is fervid and youthful, and not without considerable power of expression. . . There is, indeed, a very high religious feeling and fervour in some of these poems. Take the following on the dead Christ. . . *Si sic omnia,* this glowing young writer would be (and may yet be) one of our poets."

From the "DAILY EXPRESS" (Dublin).

" It contains much that must win the suffrages of men of educated tastes and refined sympathies. . . The healthy love of the beautiful and good, the fondness of nature, the strivings after purity and truth, which run through so many of his poems, and the ease, elegance, and force of his versification. . . There are many bright glimpses of a noble faith, and nowhere a word of mockery, of despair, or of blind misbelief. . . Some of his ideas . . . are expressed with a power and beauty which rivet the attention, and find a place in the memory."

From the "IRISH TIMES."

"Mr. ARMSTRONG is brother to him whose poems are favourites at so many homesteads, and the brother's mantle seems to have fallen upon him. . . The larger pieces are very highly finished. Through all the soul of poetry lives and breathes. The volume will undoubtedly prove a success."

From the "BELFAST NEWS-LETTER."

"This volume is Mr. GEORGE ARMSTRONG's first venture, but the public will not suffer it to be his last. . . We have, safe within these narrow covers, a work of rare power—subtle music, pure and high morality, and such true originality as is more re-markable because an occasional rhythm does recall those of our contemporary poets. . . . No competent reader of the *Remon-strance*, or *En Voyage*, or *A Love's Loss*, or *Iesus Hominum Salvator*, will be ignorant that these are the strongly personal outcome of a new mind, finding its natural, easy expression in verse, and verse of that flowing, buoyant, flexible kind, which the thought wears as lightly and unconstrained as a perfectly-fitting robe is borne. We hold this in itself to be success, and the author's justification in putting what he has to tell us into metrical form, as one who is not a rhetorician in verse, but a genuine golden poet. And this poet, having thus made good his claim, insults neither virtue nor faith by any thought which his music vivifies. If Mr. ARMSTRONG seem once or twice to be too outspoken for conventionality, he strips vice only to scourge it. . . We promise the most fastidious reader that snow will not be stained by a single verse of this volume, though blackness may possibly be made aware that it is black. The reader will learn something new of the ways and words of love and hate, sorrow of bereavement, and hope of youth, and the power of poetry to trample and to celebrate, to scorn, to woo, and to adore."

From the "OVERLAND MONTHLY" (San Francisco).

"An author of whom America will yet hear a good account."

EDMUND J. ARMSTRONG'S POEMS.

From the "TIMES," Nov. 18, 1865.

"The opening meeting of the Session 1864-65 of the Under-graduate Philosophical Society was held last evening in the dining-hall of the Dublin University, Mr. Whiteside, M.P., in the chair . . . [The] President paid a warm tribute to the memory of his predecessor, Mr. Edmund John Armstrong, now deceased, hoping that the spirit which animated him and lived in his poems might still guide and elevate members. Mr. Napier moved that the address be printed . . . He could not himself, without much emotion, listen to the affecting and beautiful tribute which the President had paid to the memory of his predecessor. He had had the privilege of moving a like resolution the previous year, when Edmund John Armstrong delivered that remarkable address to which the President alluded . . . And he trusted that that beautiful volume which, through the exertions of the Philosophical Society and of the Historical Society, had now been published, would adorn the literature of his country and tend to keep alive in their hearts the memory of one of model earnestness, of model sobriety, and of true genius. (Applause)."

"There is another gentleman, a member of this University, whose name should be maintained in eulogistic terms, and received with that profound respect which is due to his genius, his worth, and his virtues. I mean Edmund Armstrong. (Applause). He was a man of uncommon ability and undoubted talent, which gained for him the esteem, the respect, and the love of all who had the honour of knowing him. His brethren of the Historical Society have paid him the best tribute that could be paid to such an ornament of their College ; they have contributed to publish his writings to the world . . Who will not say that the poems of Edmund Armstrong are characterized by merit and excellence ? Critics have acknowledged this . . Though his life was short, yet his time was so spent and his abilities were so distinguished that he has entitled himself to the respect and gratitude of posterity. (Applause)."—SPEECH OF THE RIGHT HON. JAMES WHITESIDE, M.P., at the opening of the twenty-third Session of the Historical Society of Trinity College, Dublin.

From the "STAR," Nov. 20, 1865.

" At the opening of the Session of the Philosophical Society of Dublin University, the President pronounced a glowing panegyric on his lamented predecessor, Mr. Armstrong, whose early death has been a serious loss to literature. . . . The volume of Mr. ARMSTRONG's poems, just published, amply justifies the eulogium pronounced on that occasion. The brief memoir of a life full of promise gives us glimpses of an original and powerful character, and of very curious phases of mental struggles and discipline. . . . The poems produce an impression of striking originality, true genius, and an earnest, candid, hard-working mind."

From the "CONTEMPORARY REVIEW," March, 1866.

" A volume of the compositions of Mr. EDMUND J. ARMSTRONG has been recently given to the world. His poems . . are full of the evidences of elevated thought and keen sensibility, and moreover exhibit a faculty of refined and forcible expression, and a feeling for poetic harmony, that breathe a prophecy (not here to be fulfilled) of maturer excellence. We believe our readers will thank us for quoting as a specimen the following description of the music of the Dead March in ' Saul ' . . . With this mournful but elevating music in our ears, we pass to two other memorial notices."

From the " PUBLIC OPINION."

" This posthumous book should be prized as a memorial of the earnest labours of a singularly able thinker and writer."

From the " ATHENÆUM."

" Elegant and judicious poems."

From the " PRESS."

" Such very early flowering does not look safe ; Keats was older when he began *Endymion ;* Byron was only nineteen when he published his *Hours of Idleness,* but then they are dreadfully stupid. Such verse as Armstrong's at twenty too much resembles Bidder's calculations and Master Betty's acting . . . The two principal poems in the volume are *The Prisoner of Mount Saint Michael* and *Ovoca.* In both the fluent music of the blank-verse is marvellous for one so young . . . Some of the lyrical interludes in this poem [*Ovoca*] are very beautiful . . . The strongest poem which Mr. ARMSTRONG has written is entitled *By Gaslight.* It is too long to extract, and a few lines would give no idea of its power . . . In lieu thereof we quote a trifle which shows that the young poet had some humour."

From the " DUBLIN EVENING MAIL."

" Throughout we can recognize the true spirit of poetry and the impress of a vivid imagination. The principal piece contains beautiful and even thrilling passages . . . All are pervaded by the same vein of melancholy, here and there lightened by a steadfast faith in a higher power and another and a happier world."

From the " COURT CIRCULAR."

" There is an originality and a boldness about them which in-dicate that they are the work of one who, had he lived, would have occupied a high position . . . From the brief notice we have given of the man, it may be supposed that his writings oftentimes gave evidence of the views he so strongly held from time to time upon questions of a religious character. But this is so faint a colouring that it imbues the poetry with a mystic spirit which much enhances its value. ARMSTRONG was a true poet and for-cible. His *Prisoner of Mount Saint Michael* is full of strong dramatic effect . . . Space will only permit us to make one other quotation . . . . While it seems likewise to evidence the power of the author, it points to a faculty of expression which is very marked throughout the entire volume."

From the " GUARDIAN."

" The shorter poems . . . are of a varied character; some light and sportive, some intellectual exercises, some the agonies of a struggling soul, poured from the very depths of the writer's nature. A large number of extracts would be necessary, to give by specimen any fair notion of the collection. It will be better to recommend the whole to the attention of intelligent readers."

From the " JOHN BULL."

" Mr. ARMSTRONG's posthumous poems, the works of a talented young Irishman who was cut off in the infancy of success, exhibit in places considerable powers of writing. The *Prisoner of Mount Saint Michael,* with which the volume opens, is the passionate history of a Breton prisoner," &c. &c.

From the " LONDON REVIEW."

" There are some sweet and pretty things in his poetry, and a general tone of elegance."

From the " ART JOURNAL."

" The young poet's friends have done well in placing this wreath of *immortelles* on the tomb of the dead. It can scarcely fail to make known the name of ARMSTRONG far and wide."

From the " ATLAS."

" There are abundant traces of careful polishing and repolishing. His poems, as to their manner, are finely modulated and truly melodious. They are also serious and earnest. He abhorred all *persiflage,* and looked upon his powers and profession as a sacred trust . . . Few men at so early an age attain a style at once so well-balanced, pungent, and elegant; and the whole of his writings, whether poetical or prose, are inspired by a love of truth and a horror of wrong and wrong-doing, of a healthy and honest-hearted puritanical vehemence. . . . In such works one must generally be content if signs of promise rather than of performance are discovered. In this case we can testify to something more. These [poems] are on their own merits a sensible and substantial addition to English poetic literature. We are, on grounds identified with the interests of the commonwealth of letters, indebted to the pious care which dictated the posthumous publication of these remains of a worthy writer and a worthy man."

From the " DAILY EXPRESS " (Dublin).

" During the few months in which this volume has been before the public it has steadily advanced in the opinion of men of the finest culture and most educated taste. At first the great promise of its lamented author drew attention to the book ; now it is the book which fully reveals the greatness of the author's promise. The story has become familiar to hundreds which records his college successes, his lingering illness, his long and successful struggle for spiritual enlightenment. But neither the interest of his noble life nor the sadness of his premature removal will explain the popularity which his posthumous poems have obtained . . . Inexhaustible command of brilliant language ; boldness of metaphor, which was redeemed from extravagance by the vigilance of a fine taste ; quick and lively sympathy with many and various feelings ; an ear that was equally at home with the richest cadences of music and of verse ; an eye that rested with a lover's fervour on the shifting colours and changing shapes of beauty, alike on the face of nature and in the depths of the human soul ; and a lofty moral tone which never suffered the pure stream of meditation to be polluted—these are his claims to a place among the true poets of Great Britain."

From the " CHRISTIAN EXAMINER " (Dublin).

" The principal poem of the volume is *The Prisoner of Mount Saint Michael.* We accept it rather as a psychological poem than one which for its plot or subject can command entire sympathy, or be considered a complete success ; but looking at it as an exposition of the workings of a human soul in all its deep, passionate thoughts—love, hate, anger, tenderness, despair, terror, and finally forgiveness, resignation, hope, and joy—it has high merit. Throughout there is a masterly appreciation of the heart of man— a fine analytical power of detecting and delineating the subtle influences that sway the soul from one feeling to another ; and the progress of the mind through its various emotions, during the three days that precede the execution of the autobiographer, is wrought out with a power that proves the writer was a profound moralist and metaphysician. 'The poem abounds with fine passages, vigorous in thought, nervous in expression, and very finished in language and rhythm . . . It would be difficult to find anything more affecting in pathos, more highly wrought in its expression of intense grief, more exquisite in poetic feeling, than the verses in which Blanch bewails the death of her lover . . . The shorter pieces . . are chiefly lyrics . . . Mr. ARMSTRONG's genius was eminently lyrical, and in this species of composition he has been very successful."

From the " IRISH TIMES."

" His poetry speaks to the hearts of all who read it. Tender, passionate, thoughtful, pious, these poems are destined to live, and to hold a very high place in the literature of the age."

16

From the "FREEMAN'S JOURNAL" (Dublin).

"ARMSTRONG'S poems are among the best specimens of youthful genius that have appeared in our times, and had he lived until his thought became more compact, and time brought his exuberant imagination more under the control of reflection, there could be little doubt of his position . . . The story of the *Prisoner's* last three days is worked out with remarkable power in monologue, which would be tedious were it not for the affluence of thought and subtle knowledge of the human heart which everywhere pervade it . . . The two chief poems are in blank verse, of which there are few finer specimens in modern poetry. The minor poems in almost every page invite selection. They abound in lyrical beauty . . . Nor was the young poet deficient in observation of character and humourous expression . . . Though a ripe scholar, there is not the slightest trace of pedantry in his poetry."

From the "CONTEMPORARY REVIEW," February, 1867.

"If we were to express the chief characteristic of Mr. ARMSTRONG'S mind in a single word, we should choose the word *ardour*. In this ardour we think may be discovered the source of his strength and of his weakness. By virtue of it he was enabled to lay hold of a subject so passionately that the details could seldom fail to be worked out with vigour and sureness of touch, and we have no doubt frequently with great—perhaps too great—rapidity. By virtue of it he was borne over the formal and technical difficulties of poetry. The mastery over versification is remarkable throughout the volume from first to last—especially remarkable in a writer so young ; there is no feebleness, no flatness here ; the verse is always energetic and full . . . Ardour, vigour of imagination, mastery over versification, considerable dramatic power, ability in representing and interpreting character ; an earnest love of nature . . . These are what the reader will find in this volume . . . The arrangement of the shorter poems is much to be commended."

From a LETTER *of* M. STE-BEUVE.

" J'ai pris un douloureux plaisir à voir vivre devant moi cette jeune figure de poëte si délicate, si distinguée, si précocement douée en toutes choses . . . Il aura sa place à part, ce me semble, dans ce groupe immortel et touchant des Kirke White, des Keats ; et son jeune astre continuera de briller aux yeux de quiconque étudiera la Poésie anglaise, cette Poésie (autant que j'en puis juger) la plus riche de l'Europe moderne."

CHISWICK PRESS:—PRINTED BY WHITTINGHAM AND WILKINS, TOOKS COURT, CHANCEY LANE.